The Cottage Next Door

· · · · · · · · · ·

Books by Georgia Bockoven

THE COTTAGE NEXT DOOR

A Beach House Novella

GEORGIA BOCKOVEN

WILLIAM MORROW IMPULSE

An Imprint of HarperCollinsPublishers

THE COTTAGE NEXT DOOR. Copyright © 2015 by Georgia Bockoven. All rights reserved under International and Pan-American Copyright Conventions. By payment of the required fees, you have been granted the nonexclusive, nontransferable right to access and read the text of this e-book on screen. No part of this text may be reproduced, transmitted, decompiled, reverse-engineered, or stored in or introduced into any information storage and retrieval system, in any form or by any means, whether electronic or mechanical, now known or hereafter invented, without the express written permission of HarperCollins e-books.

EPub Edition JULY 2015 ISBN: 9780062389879
Print Edition ISBN: 9780062431639

10 9 8

Prologue

· · · · · · · · · ·

THERE WAS NO way to know the tiny heart-shaped fragment of translucent green beach glass that washed up on the shore seventy-five years ago brought a touch of magic with it. The young woman who found it had gone to the beach that morning to decide whether her life was worth living alone. She'd lost the only man she'd ever loved in a nameless battle, on a nameless island, three days before the war in the Pacific officially ended.

She didn't feel the magic right away, just a comforting sense of peace that grew to acceptance, and finally hope. The sea glass resided in the pocket of whatever pants or jackets she wore while she stayed at the cottage, a talisman she clasped when her loss threatened to return and overwhelm her. When the principal at the school where she taught fifth grade called to gently remind her that there was an upcoming mandatory staff meeting to get ready for the first day of school, she reluctantly started packing.

Distracted, she didn't notice when the sea glass slipped

from her pocket, nor did she feel it under her foot when she moved her suitcases out of the bedroom and into the enclosed back porch. She might have noticed a flash of color reflected in the sunlight when she made one more quick pass through the cottage—if only she hadn't stepped on the tiny heart again, this time tilting it on edge and forcing it between two six-inch wide pieces of rustic flooring.

She left the cottage through the back porch, stopping to look out the wall of windows that gave an unimpeded view of the cove. Something had drawn her to this room for a last good-bye, settling a sense of contentment over her as gently as one of her grandmother's silk knit shawls.

The taxi appeared ten minutes early, the driver giving two quick honks to announce his arrival. She led him to the back porch, standing to the side while he picked up three of her four suitcases. As she reached for the last bag the sun cut through the morning fog, and for an instant, out of the corner of her eye, she saw a burst of blue light. It was gone as quickly as it had appeared. Had it not been her final day, had she not been in a hurry to get to the bus depot, had the taxi driver arrived on time rather than early, she would have investigated.

Instead she forgot all about the strange blue light until she was on the Greyhound bus to Arizona, and thought to look for the glass heart in her pocket. It wasn't there. She checked her other pockets, desperately hoping she'd absentmindedly put it in one of them. But even as she looked, a voice whispered in her ear—*It's gone, leave it be.*

The heart that she had planned to make into a necklace

would have been a constant subtle reminder of the past. Letting go meant she believed, however tentatively, in her future. There might not be a new love to spend her years with, but there were friends and family and sharing and laughter.

She leaned her head against the seat cushion and stared at the mountains that rimmed the eastern edge of the long fertile San Joaquin Valley. Her thoughts drifted to the shiny new faces that would greet her in two weeks. From now on all of her energy would be focused on her fifth graders. She would encourage them to dream, and help them to fulfill their dreams.

The bus made a quick stop at a roadside restaurant. Three people got off, and one, a young soldier missing a leg, struggled to get on. Passengers greeted him as he made his way down the aisle, some thanked him for his service and sacrifice, others merely dipped their heads in acknowledgement. One white-haired man stood and saluted.

The young soldier nodded and smiled, his eyes betraying a deep weariness. Finally he reached the young woman's seat and stopped to catch his breath from his journey down the aisle. A girl, barely five, sitting two rows behind them, asked her mother about the flash of blue light—lasting less time than it takes to blink—that she saw pass between the soldier and the woman. Her mother told her it was her imagination, and went back to reading her magazine.

In Santa Cruz, the wisp of magic tucked into the sea glass settled into its new home, giving comfort to a series of owners and their infrequent renters. What happened to them wasn't so dramatic that anyone sought explanations or passed on stories that would make the cottage itself a destination. Instead, the questions that found answers, and the broken hearts that were healed, were credited to time and circumstance and luck.

While the beach house next door to the cottage sported fresh paint trim and cedar siding that was years shy of the classic faded gray, the cottage fought to keep nails in place as its wood exterior dried and shrunk with age. Inside, some rooms had been restored on a graham-cracker budget, while others reflected more prosperous times and were more like an elegant tiramisu. Tile had replaced linoleum in the bathrooms and kitchen, and the rest of the house held new hardwood floors.

Except the enclosed back porch.

For some reason, one that he'd never shared, the professional golfer who'd purchased the cottage in the middle of a career-threatening slump refused to make any changes to the porch. Not even when he'd readied the house for sale to go back on tour, and the realtor insisted the unpainted wainscoting and 1940s wallpaper would keep him from getting top dollar, did the golfer yield.

The cottage sold, and at closing, the new owners proclaimed the first thing they were going to do was remodel the porch. The golfer gave them an enigmatic smile and wished them luck.

And just as he knew would happen, nothing, with the exception of the curtains and furniture, changed. The wainscoting and wallpaper that the new owner had proclaimed hideous was suddenly charming, the floor a masterpiece of craftsmanship that provided a window to a past when hard-wood trees grew straight and strong and thick.

They don't build houses like this anymore became a mantra passed from one owner to the next. Which meant the floor in the back porch was swept and vacuumed and occasionally polished, but never replaced.

Chapter One

. . . .

JULY

THERE WAS SOMETHING about the high-pitched whine of a circular saw that made Diana Wagnor's imagination kick into overdrive. Without any real effort she pictured the man working in the house next door as someone in his late twenties, wearing a faded denim shirt with cut-off sleeves, and a weathered leather tool belt topping jeans slung low on his hips.

Of course it was a given that living in California he'd have sun-bleached hair, six-pack abs, and a killer smile. Oh, and dark blue eyes with long curling eyelashes.

Great eyes were a must in her fantasy of what went into creating the perfect man. Not only was it important that they be beautiful, they should be playful and sexy at the same time. Oh, and filled with a sensual promise, but that went hand in hand with sexy.

Diana let out a frustrated sigh. What insanity—to swear off men for two years and then purposely wallow in vision of a construction worker. Until she found a reason to trust her own judgment again, he could be the guy who checked off every detail on her imaginary list of what went into the perfect man, and she still wouldn't do anything about it.

For someone who'd lived her entire life in the geographical center of the United States, seeing the ocean for the first time was tantamount to seeing Neil Armstrong's footprint on the moon. And yet here she was, sitting on a deck with a view most people saved for honeymoons or special anniversaries, except she was alone. If only she'd come to California less burdened, the pleasure would have been more joyful. But broken hearts were heavy, and she was worn out carrying hers.

How was it that she'd never fallen for anyone who hadn't disappointed her in the end or who had bailed when the road turned rocky?

Her first real boyfriend, Louis Bickford, had eyes that triggered fantasies far too complex for a naive thirteen-year-old to understand. They were a couple, or at least a couple in her mind, right up to the day he asked Judy Feldman to the graduation dance. Too embarrassed to tell her mother what had really happened, Diana faked a stomach flu and sobbed her way through the weekend.

What followed all the way through high school and into college was a string of drop-dead gorgeous "bad boys"—the only kind that ever held her attention past hello.

Would she never learn?

By her junior year at the University of Kansas, after she'd discovered her latest boyfriend had been tossed out of school for cheating on a final, Diana had a talk with her favorite sibling, her oldest brother Brian. She poured out her heart to him, reciting a list of loser boyfriends, ending with a tearful diatribe against men.

Brian listened patiently and then gave her one of his succinct always on-point answers. Plain and simple, the problem wasn't men—it was her unerring ability to zero in on the worst ones. For whatever screwy reason, she found these supposedly misunderstood antiheroes sexy, believing all they lacked to turn their lives around was the love of a good woman.

Her.

Ha.

Diana drove back to Lawrence determined to change. And she did. For a week. Right up to the moment her roommate introduced her to Howard Clausen.

He was tall and muscular, a long-distance swimmer on the varsity team, with short brown hair that begged to have fingers run through it. His eyes were a soft electric blue, the lashes thick and curling. Best of all he was smart and articulate, and someone she actually wanted to introduce to her parents. The total package.

He was also the reason, seven years later, that she'd left the only home she'd ever known and moved to California, that she had zero balances in both her saving and retirement accounts, that she owned a bare lot where the house her great-grandfather had built with his own hands had once stood, and that she'd sworn off men.

Not forever, of course. She had sense enough to know that

forever wasn't in her genetic makeup. Two years had seemed like a good compromise. She'd be thirty-one by then and hopefully imbued with the wisdom that came with age. She would be able to look at an Abercrombie & Fitch model and recognize that until he proved he was more than a pretty face, all he had going for him was packaging.

Six months down. Eighteen to go.

Letting out a frustrated sigh, she leaned back in an Adirondack chair in need of a coat of varnish. The wooden deck of her cousin Cheryl's beach cottage went half the length of the back of the house, and provided a perfect private view of the ocean. At least being here had lived up to her expectations. The waves and white sand, even the noisy seagulls and salty air were exactly as she'd pictured them. From the minute she'd pulled into the driveway and stopped to stare into the seemingly endless horizon, she'd been overcome with the feeling that if she had to leave her beloved Kansas to escape her past, she was exactly where she belonged.

Her phone vibrated on the glass top of the wicker table beside her. For a second she considered not even looking to see who it was and letting the call go to voice mail. Then she remembered her mother had said she would call before she left for her planning committee meeting. Despite Andrew and Cheryl's reassurances that Diana would be staying in a nice neighborhood with great neighbors, in a reasonably large house that, incidentally, just happened to have a million dollar view of the Pacific Ocean, her mother had a compulsive need to find something to worry about.

"Hey, Mom. What's up?" Diana tucked the phone between

her shoulder and chin, and went inside to get a glass of the iced tea she'd made earlier.

Jenny Wagnor laughed. "You mean since I called you last night?"

Diana was the first of Jenny's five children to move more than an hour-and-a-half drive from Topeka. Although her mother put on a good front, she was having a hard time coping with her youngest being two entire time zones away. "It's okay, Mom. I miss you, too."

"It's not fair that you're the one who had to leave."

No, it wasn't, but "fair" had never been part of the dialogue in her breakup with Howard. After the fire, because she had no where else to go, Diana had moved in with her parents, insisting to her hovering mother that she was only there temporarily, just until she was back on her feet again.

What was supposed to be weeks turned into months. Promising job interviews turned into minimum wage positions with no future prospects or current benefits.

In the beginning Howard had texted hourly, emailed constantly, and finally screwed up the courage to call. When nothing worked he stupidly came to her parents' house, carrying an enormous bouquet and insisting he be allowed to see Diana. For a minute, when her mother actually accepted the bouquet, his appeal appeared to be working. Then he must have said something that didn't sit right because her mother abruptly took the stem ends and wielded the flowers like a baseball bat, driving Howard off the porch and back to his car, his exit marked by a rainbow of fragrant fluttering petals.

Diana actually laughed out loud. It was the first time she'd laughed since the fire.

She missed laughing, and smiling, and feeling good about herself. Her mother insisted all she needed was time. When Diana inevitably rolled her eyes in response, Jenny insisted it wasn't just an expression, that time really did heal all wounds.

Maybe your normal run-of-the-mill disappointment that comes with being turned down for a new car loan—but not the kind of wound Howard had inflicted. It was too big and too ugly. Diana would carry the scar the rest of her life.

She started going through the unfamiliar cupboards, looking for sugar to put in her iced tea.

"So, how is it?" Jenny asked. "The house, I mean."

Diana made a grab for the phone when it slipped from under her chin. Jenny had asked the same question the night before but plainly wasn't satisfied with Diana's answer. "Actually, it feels like home. Cheryl collects teapots. There's a shelf in the kitchen filled with them. Or I guess it could be Andrew who collects them. What do you think? Does he seem like the teapot-collecting type?"

"It's Cheryl. She got them from Grandma Marge."

Unsuccessful in her cupboard sugar quest, Diana leaned her hip against the counter and glanced around the kitchen for something that looked like it might hold sugar. "I think you'd like Andrew, Mom. There are pictures of him and Cheryl and the kids all over the place. Not just snapshots—really good pictures. He looks like a nice guy." She could have added that they looked like an insurance company ad depicting the perfect married couple, but that seemed a little too

much. "And Bobby looks like a handful. What is he, eigh
years old now?"

"Seven and a half, going on sixteen, according to Cheryl
You probably don't remember this but Rebecca, their oldes
daughter, is a professional photographer. Cheryl and Andrew
are so proud of her for snagging that job with the Nationa
Park Service, especially considering the competition she had."

"Ah—I forgot." Diana wasn't proud of the twinge of jeal
ousy she felt over Rebecca's job success, especially consider
ing it was undoubtedly something she'd accomplished on he
own without the help of family contacts.

"She was the reason they all went to Botswana thi
summer and you wound up with a place to stay rent free
Cheryl said she figured it was their last chance to go as a
family. I told you about this already. Remember?"

She didn't, at least not all of it. Mainly because her mothe
had a habit of choosing the worst possible times to tell he
things, like in the middle of the detective announcing who'
committed the murder on Diana's favorite television show. I
was as if her mother had a finite time to say something befor
it was lost forever, and nothing was going to get in her way.

Her gaze settled on a ceramic pot decorated with hand
painted orchids sitting beside a salt and pepper shaker. Suc
cess. "I do remember you saying they were adopting anothe
baby when they got home. How many does this make?"

"Including the baby, four, plus a half-dozen foster chil
dren."

"Do you think I could talk them into adopting me? I lov
this place."

"Already?"

"Just wait until you come for a visit. You'll understand."

"I was afraid that was going to happen. Since you were a little girl you've been drawn to water." Jenny paused. "That's my ride. Gotta go, sweetheart. I'll call you tonight."

Her mother was deep into her fifteenth year of organizing the annual three-day women's retreat at church. She'd miss an entire week of *Days of Our Lives* before she'd be five minutes late to one of their meetings.

"Have fun." She hit the off button and stuffed the phone in her back pocket.

Glancing up from putting her spoon in the sink, Diana let out a startled gasp. Nose pressed to the window, staring at her as if she were an ice cream cone on a hundred-degree day, were slightly offset brown eyes, accompanied by a pair of floppy ears, and a mouth lifted into a wide version of a canine smile. The second Diana made eye contact, a pink tongue appeared and the head bobbed in excitement.

Chapter Two

....

DIANA STOOD ON the front porch of the beach house next door to Cheryl and Andrew's cottage and peered through the open door. "Hello?"

The construction worker she'd imagined earlier pulled aside a plastic tarp hanging from the ceiling at the back of the house. Her jaw dropped in surprise. It was as if her older brother, Brian, had been cloned.

"Can I help you?" he asked, acknowledging her peculiar reaction with a puzzled frown.

"I'm staying over there—" She pointed toward Andrew's house. "There's this dog that seems to be lost and I was wondering if you might know who she belongs to." She thought a second. "At least I think it's a 'she.' Or it could be a 'he.' To be honest, I didn't look."

"What kind of dog?" he asked in a way that suggested he already knew.

"About so tall—" She indicated knee-high. "Light reddish

brown. Friendly. Floppy ears. Mixed breed." As if on cue, the dog appeared at Diana's side, its tail shifting into high gear at the sight of the man.

He wiped his hands on his jeans and followed a paper path to the front door. "She's mine." He crouched down and cupped the dog's muzzle, forcing her to look at him. "What do you have to say for yourself?"

As deflated as a football in a playoff game, she dropped her head and let out a soft whine. Contradicting the contrite posture, her tail never stopped swinging.

He offered Diana an apologetic smile. "She's looking for my daughter and your cousin Bobby. The three of them have been constant companions this summer and she doesn't understand why they've seemingly abandoned her. I hate to tie her up, but it looks like I'm going to have to."

"Does she always come to work with you?" There was a missing piece to this puzzle.

"Only when my daughter Shiloh is in school or staying with someone. Coconut accepts me, but she's really Shiloh's dog." He gave Coconut's floppy ears a final scratch, stood, and steered the dog toward the room behind the tarp.

"How did you know who I—" She made a dismissive wave. "Never mind—I know. Cheryl told you I was coming."

He smiled. "Not just me. Everyone in the cove has been told to be on the lookout for you."

"Sounds like something my mother would do." While it didn't thrill her to know she was being watched, her mother would rest easier.

He held out his hand. "Jeremy Richmond—permanent

resident of Santa Cruz, transient here in the cove until I've finished rebuilding this kitchen."

"Diana Wagnor—possible permanent resident of Santa Cruz, depending on how my new job works out. But after looking at the real estate flyer I picked up last night, I can say without hesitation that I'm a temporary resident of the cove." The price of a bungalow half the size of the house she'd burned to the ground in Topeka cost ten times as much in the cove; she could only imagine the rental price. What appeared to be an ordinary house that also had an ocean view, but was in another part of the city, would buy the Governor's Mansion sitting on five hundred acres back home.

"I meant to stop by last night to introduce myself and Shiloh, but it didn't work out."

"I'm sorry I missed her." She looked around the tarp-covered living room. "I love construction projects. Would you mind showing me what you're doing? I happen to be one of those obnoxious home improvement junkies."

"Right now there's not a lot to see beyond a gutted room and a set of plans." He moved to the side to make room for her to step onto the paper that covered the hardwood floor. "Are you into the *This Old House* kind of home improvement, or the rebuild a three-thousand-square-foot house in a weekend kind?"

She laughed. "You're talking to a woman whose first crush was on Norm Abram. I was devastated when *The New Yankee Workshop* was canceled."

"Then you should appreciate what Julia has hired me to do in this kitchen remodel."

"Julia's the homeowner?"

He reached around her to move aside the hanging tarp. "To her it's more than a home. It's a love affair."

Diana went to the newly installed triple-paned window and looked outside. If this were her home, she'd never use the dishwasher, not when she could stand at a sink with such a view. "You have the perfect job."

"Why's that?"

"Building houses and doing it here."

"I do more rebuilding than building nowadays. The last house I built from the foundation up was a dozen years ago." He rolled out the kitchen plans on a sawhorse table. "This is the second time I've worked on this house. And the first time on any project I've done that I'm glad to get a chance at a do-over."

Diana held her hands behind her and looked at the plans. "In what way are you glad?"

"The first go-round was top-of-the-line everything, and wound up too modern and too flashy. The style didn't fit a hundred-year-old house. It needed a ceramic farm sink, not stainless steel, and a subway tile backsplash, not gray and blue art glass. Then there was a leak that did major water damage and Julia got to start over. It took a year of planning and scheduling, but we finally got together."

Coconut came on point, stood with her head cocked for several seconds, then bent down to crawl under the tarp, her tail whipping around like a lopsided helicopter blade.

"Where is everyone?" A deep male voice came from the direction of the front door.

"Excuse me," Jeremy said to Diana. "That's Michael with my lunch."

Even though it was too much of a coincidence, her first impulse was to ask, "Michael Williams?"

He nodded before he pushed aside the tarp. Diana caught a glimpse of the man she'd be working with at the galleries for the next month—until Peter, the artist who owned the galleries, returned from Europe. She still wasn't sure whether she was working "with" or "for" Michael, only that he was in charge of the day-to-day operation and would be able to answer her bookkeeping questions.

She moved so that she could see him better through the slit in the opening Jeremy left behind. She guessed Michael to be around her age, give or take a year or so. He was the same height as Jeremy, with black wavy hair and dark green eyes that appeared to be flecked with brown, and reminded her of the boys she'd grown up with in Kansas who worked on their family cattle ranches. Their bodies were hard and lean, their physical abilities exhibited in a quiet confidence and in the self-assured way they moved. Wearing low-slung jeans and a blue tee shirt with a whale fading into oblivion, Michael had an enigmatic look about him that said he'd be as comfortable straddling a Harley as sitting behind the wheel of a Ferrari.

It was tempting to think Peter wouldn't leave his business in the hands of someone incompetent, but it wasn't unheard of for family ties to trump good sense. More than one son had run his father's business into bankruptcy.

Jeremy took the white bag and pointed to the box. "What's this?"

MICHAEL WILLIAMS STRAIGHTENED from petting Coconut, who immediately moved to sit on his foot and look up at him adoringly. "You should have known I couldn't pick up your lunch without getting Shiloh one of her favorite chocolate cookies. Because I was feeling generous, there's a macaroon in there for you."

"You spoil her, Michael." Jeremy took the box and put it on a plastic-covered dining room table. "And me. I'll make sure she gets this tonight."

"Is she with Rosa?" The question was a form of code between them, and didn't require an answer. Rosa was the visiting nurse who stayed with Shiloh when she wasn't doing well.

Michael had known Jeremy and Shiloh for almost ten years, starting the summer his mother married Peter Wylie, and Peter hired Jeremy to add a bedroom to his house.

The bonds he'd formed with Shiloh when she was two years old and he was nineteen were accidental. The only toddler he'd had anything to do with up to then was his uncle's little girl. She was a holy terror who'd poured a soda over the keyboard of his laptop when the sound wouldn't work on her favorite movie, *Finding Nemo*.

Figuring all kids that age were alike, Michael did everything possible to stay away from Shiloh, even questioning his mother's sanity for taking on her care when she and Peter had just come home from their honeymoon.

But Shiloh had a way about her that shattered his defenses. He became her favorite, the one she went to with outstretched arms when she needed comforting, the one whose hand she reached for when they went to the beach to look for seashells, the one she clung to at the doctor's office whenever her lupus came back like a ferocious wounded lion and left her in excruciating pain.

She became the sister he'd never had. He became her defender, fiercely protective and at times insanely angry at a mother who had decided she wasn't cut out to be the parent of a child with a life-threatening illness.

After a year of withdrawing both emotionally and physically, Shiloh's mother had abandoned her adopted daughter and Jeremy, leaving Jeremy with a critically ill two-year-old who just weeks earlier had been diagnosed with systemic lupus erythematosus, an incurable, complicated, and multifaceted disease. Without help to care for her, Jeremy told his clients that he was not going to be able to finish the jobs he'd started, and promised he would put them in touch with other contractors and reimburse them for their losses as soon as he was able.

That was when Michael's mother stepped in, becoming a surrogate mother to Shiloh and a layman expert on children with SLE for Jeremy.

Jeremy ran his hand through his hair, dislodging bits of sawdust. "It's her knees again. She said she was feeling great, but that Rosa needed company because the rest of her family was in Mexico."

It was all Jeremy needed to say. Michael had gone through years of Shiloh's bouts of severe joint pain, making a game out of carrying her on his back when it hurt too much for her to walk by herself. He'd never told anyone, but Shiloh was instrumental in his decision to attend the University of California, Santa Cruz, rather than Berkeley for his undergraduate degree in marine biology, and the real reason he'd come home to run the galleries every summer when he'd moved to San Diego to get his master's degree.

Coconut shifted to Michael's other foot and leaned against his leg, tilting up her muzzle for a scratch. "She must be going nuts without either of the kids around."

"She sneaked out earlier and went next door. Diana saw her and thought she was either lost or abandoned." At Michael's confused expression, Jeremy added, "Your new accountant? The one who's staying in Cheryl and Andrew's house?"

Michael felt a look bordering on panic cross his face. "She wasn't supposed to be here until next week." He stared at the ceiling and let out a groan of frustration. "I guess I should go over and introduce myself."

"No need. She's in the kitchen."

"*Shit*," Michael said under his breath. Having her show up a week early was the last thing he needed.

Chapter Three

· · · · · · · · ·

IF JOB PROFILING still existed—one of those ancient social
mores where everyone automatically assumed a doctor was
male and the owner of a day care business was female—
Michael stepped into the cliché with both feet when Jeremy
introduced him to Diana Wagnor. He stared at her in tongue-
tied disbelief. She was not what he'd imagined a woman who
made her living balancing checkbooks and tracking invoices
would look like.

Embarrassed by how readily he'd stereotyped her, automatically expecting a younger version of Hester Savage, the
sixty-three-year-old woman who'd kept the books for Peter
since he'd opened his first gallery twenty years ago, Michael
mentally filed it away under lessons learned. Not that he was
disappointed she was a Jennifer Lawrence double. Powerful, confident women defined sexy in his personal diction-
ary. Give him a woman who looked as if she could take on an
army with a bow and a quiver full of arrows, and he was hers

"Hi—Diana Wagnor," she said, coming forward and shaking his hand. "I'm early, but I figured it would be helpful if I got a feel for the town and people before I jumped in."

"First time in California?" Michael asked.

She nodded. "First time I've seen an ocean." A broad smile accompanied the statement. "I'm impressed."

"Michael Williams," he said, liking that she shook his hand, and not just his fingers, and captivated by a smile that lit her entire face. "That makes us even. Kind of. I've never been to Kansas."

"Doesn't surprise me. It's one of those states most people only see from the air."

Michael looked around at what had been a kitchen a month ago, noting the new lumber on the outside wall. "Couldn't save any of the old stuff?" he said to Jeremy.

"There were only two studs that I felt confident using so I decided to go with all new, and save what I could for that section of decking that needs replacing."

"So what's next?"

"The electrician is coming this afternoon to put in a new service panel and run another line for the lights Julia wants over the island. In the meantime I have to try to track down the contractor who picked up my tile by accident and then took off on vacation to Mexico."

"Which sounds like my cue to get out of here and let you get to it."

"I'd like to try to catch him before he's so far in the country that he loses cell service."

Diana moved toward the tarp. "Would it be all right if I

came over once in awhile to see how it's going? I promise not to take up too much of your time."

"Come over anytime. And I'm sorry about Coconut bugging you. I'll leave her home tomorrow."

"Oh, please don't. If it's okay with you and Shiloh, I'd like to take her running with me while I'm staying at the cottage. I could use the company."

Michael looked at Jeremy and rolled his eyes. "I'm going to have to figure out how that dog wraps everyone she meets around that big hairy paw of hers."

"Going to take lessons?" Jeremy leaned against the doorframe.

"Hell, yes." Michael headed toward his car, then stopped, feeling guilty about not being more welcoming to Diana. There was no way she could know how much more complicated she'd made his life by showing up a week early. "Are you hungry?"

"I don't know. I'm still on Kansas time." She looked at her watch.

"And?"

She flashed such an enthusiastic smile that it compounded his guilt.

"Turns out I am," she said.

Jeremy laughed. "Smooth, Michael. By the way, thanks for the cookies. Shiloh will be sorry she missed you."

Chapter Four

· · · · · · · · · ·

THE DELI MICHAEL took Diana to had customers snaking out the door and lining the sidewalk. "Popular place," she said.

She expected him to keep going to find somewhere less crowded, but he drove his Prius around the block twice, patiently waiting for a parking space to open.

"It's one of the few places the locals don't abandon when the tourists arrive," he said. "Which means you either put up with the crowds or settle for second best."

"That's impressive." She leaned forward to get a better look into an alley they were passing.

Spotting a car with its backup lights on, Michael stopped and signaled to the driver of the truck behind him to go around. The driver flipped them off as he passed.

Diana was dumbfounded when Michael laughed and waved, casually dismissing something the guys her age back home would have taken as a challenge. "Is that some Santa Cruz thing, turning the other cheek?"

He seemed truly surprised by her question. "He's an outlander. I try to make allowances for them."

"How can you tell he's—what did you call him?"

"Outlander. It's something my brother and I came up with when we were kids. You'll understand when you've been here awhile. The only thing that upsets the people who live here is seeing someone trashing the place." He gave her a teasing smile. "Then look out. That little old lady who invites strangers in for tea and cookies can turn on a dime."

"You're one of those people, I take it?" Her friends had warned her about California and its left-of-center population, insisting she would never fit in and would be home by Christmas. What they didn't know was how desperate she was to make this work. She was twenty-nine years old, with a string of failed relationships and not one decent job offer in Topeka. She needed *something* to work.

"I think it's more that I'm the son of a preacher man."

Really? Diana was sure Cheryl hadn't mentioned that in addition to his painting, Peter was a minister. At least not to her. She glanced at him, tossing off an easy smile. "Back home they were the kids who always got into trouble."

"Probably because they didn't have someone like my mother taking care of them. She could make a boot camp drill sergeant look like a Girl Scout leader."

The car they'd been waiting for jockeyed free of the tight parking space. The driver smiled and waved as she drove by. "She would be a local," Diana guessed, playing along.

"Who also happens to be a friend." They approached the restaurant, but instead of going to the back of the line, he pu his hand on her shoulder and guided her inside to the hand-written menu hanging on the wall behind the counter. The woman taking orders at the cash register looked up, spotted Michael, and gave him a huge grin.

"Hey, Michael, where you been?" she called. "The pastra-mi's just the way you like it, nice and lean."

"Thanks, Naomi." He pointed to Diana. "I brought you a new customer—all the way from Kansas."

"Welcome," she called to Diana as she added an order to a wire that traveled the length of the prep area. "I hope we don't disappoint you. California is a long way to come for a deli sandwich, especially with New York so close."

"Michael told me the delis in New York can't hold a candle to yours."

Naomi put her fingers to her lips and blew them a kiss.

"Nice one," Michael said, leaning into Diana so she could hear him without shouting. "Now comes the hard part."

It took almost ten minutes to settle on what had been her first choice, corned beef on rye and an enormous Kosher dill pickle. After doing some quick calorie calculating, and tell-ing herself she would settle for an undressed wedge salad for dinner, she added a root beer milkshake. She'd lost twenty pounds in the too-sick-to-her-stomach-to-eat diet that came with having her world fall apart, and it wasn't something she wanted to go through again just to fit into her new wardrobe.

Rather than go back outside and wait in line to place their order, Michael took out his phone and called it in. "It's something Naomi does for her regulars. There are a couple of workers in the back who take care of all the phone orders, so depending on how many people called in before us, we should be on our way in half the time."

Fifteen minutes later they were out the door and on their way to West Cliff Drive to see if they could snag a bench on the walkway to eat their lunch and watch the surfers.

"I DIDN'T EXPECT there would be an ocean smell," Diana said, tilting her cup to gather the last drops of milkshake before putting it into the bag they'd used for their empty wrappers. "It's not exactly fishy, it's more salty, but it's something else, too."

Michael shrugged. "I've never given it any real thought. All I know is that when I've been away, I like the way it smells when I come home." He made a grab for a napkin that was about to take flight. "What's Topeka like?"

"I don't know . . . like any other city, I guess. It's when you get out in the country that things are different. Everything there is tied to the seasons—turned earth in the spring and harvesting the wheat in late summer. I think I'll miss the growing season most of all. I was sure there couldn't be anything more beautiful than the wind sweeping across a wheat field, but that was before I saw the ocean."

"I have no idea where they grow wheat around here, but the Salinas Valley is only a few miles away. You can get an entire salad there, from fancy lettuce to mushrooms and tomatoes. Plus, there's artichokes and Brussels sprouts."

"Oh, yum."

He laughed. "Sounds like you'll be skipping the farmers

markets around here. If you want to see something beautiful grown in greenhouses, there's always Andrew's orchids."

"He promised to give me a full tour when they get back from Botswana." Diana twisted sideways to face Michael, bringing one leg up to tuck under the other. "Have you always lived here?"

"The answer to that has a lot of *Penny Dreadful* elements to it. Are you sure you want to hear it?"

"*Penny Dreadful*—how fun. I haven't heard that term since my freshman lit class." A breeze caught the strand of her curly shoulder-length hair that refused to stay tucked behind her ear, and whipped it across her face. Impatient with the battle, she gave up and reached into her purse for an elastic band, finger combing the mass into a ponytail.

"I'll give you the abbreviated version or we'd be here the rest of the day, and you'd be making up places you had to be." He leaned back and put his hands behind his head. "My family first rented the house that Jeremy's working on when I was a kid. We'd stay there one month every summer. For a long time I thought one of Dad's parishioners owned it and cut us a deal, but it was my mom who'd found it through a friend of hers. She loves the ocean more than almost anyone else I know. And she was happier here than she ever was at home."

"Almost?" It seemed a strange qualifier.

"Shiloh tops the list. After she's been cooped up in the hospital, you can see a physical change come over her when she returns home again. Unlike most people, she really likes it when there are clouds or storms or fog. That's the only time she doesn't have to protect herself from the sun."

"Is she in the hospital a lot?"

"She has a particularly bad form of lupus that hasn't left her a lot of time in remission. Depending on where it manifests itself in her body, she could be in the hospital more than out."

He took his phone out of his pocket and looked at it on the off chance he'd missed the text from Peter setting up their phone call about what to do with Diana. The nine-hour time difference made connecting difficult, but this was something that couldn't be put off, especially now that she'd shown up a whole week early. The longer they waited to tell Diana that she might not have a job after all, the harder it would be.

"Am I keeping you from something?" Diana asked.

"Sorry—I'm expecting a call." He shoved the phone back in his pocket. "Where were we?"

"You were telling me about Shiloh coming home from the hospital."

One day, if Diana stuck around after what they were going to do to her, he would introduce her to Shiloh. He had a feeling they were alike in a lot of ways and that they'd slip into a friendship as easily as Jeremy joined complex miter joints. "I'm sorry. I forgot you didn't know her."

"So you stayed at the beach house every summer," she offered instead of pursuing information about Shiloh.

"Over the years we got to know most of the people who lived in the cove. One was Peter Wylie. It wasn't until I was in high school and saw something he'd painted hanging in my girlfriend's house that I discovered he wasn't just a local artist who sold pictures to tourists—he was world-famous."

"I'm confused. I thought Peter Wylie was your father. When you said you were the son of a preacher, I just assumed he gave up his church to become an artist."

Michael laughed. "He's my mother's second husband, and about as far away from being a preacher as you can get. I wasn't kidding when I said this gets complicated."

Diana was reluctant to admit that she'd never heard of Peter Wylie until Cheryl called and said there was a book-keeping job opening at his galleries, and would she like to move to California to work for him? Peter scheduled a Skype interview from the Italian villa he had rented in Italy that left her excited and hopeful.

They settled on the wage and benefit package, and she was hired. Just like that, she was working again. It felt good. No, it felt wonderful. Someone wanted her.

She'd texted him several times with questions, and despite a killer itinerary filled with meet and greet sessions at galleries scattered throughout seven countries, he always got back to her within a day.

She liked Peter and wished she could continue learning the business from him, instead of Michael. He'd been easy to talk to and up-front about the fact that one of his galleries—the one that specialized in prints and lithographs—was in financial trouble and might have to be closed. Her first responsibility would be to look for ways to stem the bleeding, and if that couldn't be done, then to figure out the best way to close the doors with as little consequence to their employees, vendors, and the neighborhood as possible.

The idea that she would be using skills she'd learned in

her forensic accounting classes excited her. Up to now her entire career had centered on standard accounting practices, and there were times she seriously doubted she'd make it to retirement without finding a way to clear the cobwebs from her mind. She couldn't wait to get started on the Santa Cruz gallery's books. Especially since, according to Peter, the Carmel gallery was in good shape, requiring little more than standard bookkeeping.

"I like complicated," she said.

"Without going into a lot of boring detail—"

But she loved detail. You had to be a detail person to be a bookkeeper. She smiled. "You're not boring me. With all the baggage I've been carrying lately, it's refreshing to hear about someone else's."

Michael no longer questioned why he was telling her intimate details of his life. It was his screwed up way to show her that what was about to happen had nothing to do with her, that he and Peter were responsible.

"My dad was going through a midlife crisis and decided he and my mother needed to spend some time apart. That morphed into him deciding he wanted a divorce, which made it a little tricky to convince the congregation that he was still the good guy. He knew what kind of gossip was making the rounds about my mother, but he did nothing to protect her. Instead, he acted like the wounded party and accepted all the cakes and casseroles and offers to do laundry that came with the tea and sympathy. Then he woke up one morning and decided God didn't want him to get a divorce after all."

"And in the meantime your mother had moved on with

her life." The scenario was one she'd pictured for herself in a hundred different ways. Instead, her ego was still bleeding. She was tired of all the bandaging it required, but couldn't seem to move on.

"Not quite. She landed feet first into her own set of complications. It turned out that Peter had been in love with my mother from the first day he met her. When he found out that she and my father were getting a divorce, he figured it was now or never and finally told her how he felt."

"Wow," she said. "And?"

"She'd never thought of him that way. Actually, she'd always believed he was single because he was gay."

"You're kidding." But before he could say anything, she added, "No, it makes perfect sense. Where I grew up it's not possible for a preacher's wife to have a close male friend any other way. Peter had to be gay. At least in her mind."

Michael shifted positions, leaning forward and putting his elbows on his knees. "But he wasn't."

"You didn't like Peter back then, I take it?" she said carefully. In high school several of her friends' parents had gotten divorced, and every one of them wound up blaming the new spouse, logic be damned.

"I liked him a lot actually. But it took a while before we became friends." He looked at Diana and smiled. "Real friends, not the lip service kind. I just regret how screwed up my dad's life has been since he decided to drag my mother through his midlife crisis. He didn't take it well when she refused to come back for more.

"Eventually the deacons gently suggested he find another

place to spread God's word. He surprised us all when he accepted an offer from a small church in Montana. I don't think he paid attention to the 'small' part in the letter, only the part about how long they'd gone without guidance and how much they needed him. Turned out the majority of the membership considered attending services on Christmas and Easter was all God expected or wanted from them. He gets by on the kindness of the women who bring him food from their gardens and eggs from their chickens, and the rancher who tithes with a side of beef every year."

"And your mother? Is she happy?"

"Deliriously—her word, not mine." He turned to look at Diana. "She says she found her soul mate."

"Ouch. That must have been hard for your dad to hear." With all the pain that came with a breakup, none was as sharp or deep as seeing an ex-partner truly happy. "Did you still see him a lot after he moved?"

He sat up straight again, reaching for their garbage bag and folding the top. "About as often as his congregation— Christmas and Easter. He wants me to move to Montana, but I'm a Californian, through and through. I can't imagine what I'd do living back there."

"I was so sure when I was growing up that I would get out of Kansas as soon as I could. I've had a case of wanderlust from the day I read my first *Ranger Rick* magazine at the dentist's office."

He looked at her with new interest. "Where have you lived?"

"Everywhere—" she laughed. "In my mind, that is. In

reality, this is the first time I've been to a state that doesn't border Kansas."

"That's a start."

"How many states have you been in?"

"Twenty-seven. It's not as impressive as it sounds. I have relatives on the east coast, where you can hit five states in a day. Most of the rest came from a trip I took with my brother a few years back."

"I'm wondering whether I have it in me to stay away from everything I've known and everyone I love." She realized the minute it was out that she'd made a mistake. Giving Michael the impression she had doubts about whether or not she would stay in California wasn't the way to instill confidence in Peter's decision to hire her.

"I don't mean that the way it sounds. It's just that Topeka has over a hundred thousand people, but block by block, church by church, neighborhood by neighborhood, it's like living in a small town. One where everyone looks out for each other. I'm going to miss that."

"California has absorbed too many cultures to be known for anything but diversity. There are communities out here that are like Topeka. But there are some that encourage independence and have people who spend an entire lifetime living next door to someone they never meet."

"I would go nuts living in a neighborhood like that." She put her hands on her knees and stood, taking the bag from Michael and heading toward the garbage can.

It was obvious she'd planned to come back, but Michael followed her, deciding it was a good time to leave.

They moved to the curb and waited for traffic to clear. "Is the gallery near here?"

He pointed north. "A couple of blocks that way."

"Would you mind driving by on the way back? I'd love to see it." Before she took the job, she did an Internet search for Peter Wylie's work, and was relieved to discover she liked it. She couldn't imagine spending five days a week surrounded by the works of a Jackson Pollock wannabe.

When he didn't answer right away, she remembered seeing him check his watch earlier. "Sorry—I forgot you were expecting a call. I don't have anything to do this afternoon. I can come back later."

Taking her to the gallery when it was possible she would never work there seemed downright mean. Of course he could be wrong about how all of this was going to end. Hell, he could be wrong about everything.

He absently touched her arm, forming a connection as they crossed the street. He was only a couple of days away from becoming the world's biggest jerk, or close to it. When that happened, she was going to wish she'd never heard of California, or Santa Cruz, or Peter Wylie Galleries. The least he could do was give her a couple of good memories before the bubble burst.

He opened her door and moved around the car. "There's not much to see. It won't take long."

Chapter Five

· · · · · · · · ·

THE PICTURES OF the gallery didn't do it justice. The building was a block from the ocean, but easily accessible to those drawn off the beaten path by the lure of a historic home constructed to look like a lighthouse. She could see why the gallery would appeal to anyone looking for an out-of-the-ordinary souvenir of their trip to Santa Cruz. Instead of the typical hats and tee shirts and seashell frames she'd seen yesterday in the shop next to the grocery store, they could have a limited edition print of a painting by the area's premier artist.

The body of the building was painted a Carolina blue, the shutters a medium grey, the trim an off-white. The shingles that covered the tower sported a darker weathered gray, the optic section at the very top of the tower was a circle of green-tinted glass panes. A narrow walkway with a sturdy metal railing surrounded the lookout.

Diana tried to take it all in from where they'd parked at

the back of the building, but had to move to the front to see everything.

A ten-foot-wide section of grass ran the length of the building, with flowerbeds tucked against the house and behind the white picket fence. A classically simple sign hung over the gate—*Peter Wylie Gallery*.

"Nice," Diana said, her tone carrying more appreciation than the word.

"You should have seen this place when my mother found it. She was the only one who could see its potential. Even Peter called it a money pit in the making, and he thinks my mom is the most brilliant person he knows."

"What happened?"

"Jeremy."

"Beach house Jeremy?"

"The same. It took him almost a year but he turned what everyone considered a teardown into a place listed in all the tours of Santa Cruz."

"Can't ask for better advertising."

"They hoped the lithographs and limited edition prints would work well in this market— they just didn't have any idea how well."

"And then it all fell apart this past year?" she asked, repeating what Peter had told her.

"More like a year and a half," he said.

"And you have no idea why?" If she weren't days away from a job where it would be up to her to look for an answer she never would have asked the question.

"We're working on it." His tone made it clear he didn't want to talk about it anymore.

At his abrupt answer, the follow-up questions she'd wanted to ask stuck in her throat.

Michael dug out his keys, and opened the front door. Diana followed him inside and waited while he disengaged the alarm. To the right, in what had once been a bedroom in the converted house, was a small office with puzzlingly old computer equipment. Three tall file cabinets sat side by side on the back wall, pre-cloud storage relics. Diana subscribed to copying and storing on redundant cloud systems, followed by the use of a good crosscut shredding company after the legal limit had been reached on disposable audit documents. She had a strong suspicion there were records that went back twenty years or more that were mixed in with important current information, all vulnerable to flood and fire and theft. Warning bells went off, their tolling louder than the Vatican on Easter morning.

"This will be your office," he said. "Hester has it set up so that she works here Monday, Wednesday, and Friday, and then Tuesday and Thursday in the Carmel Gallery, but that's just her way of doing things, not anything set in stone. Feel free to do what works best for you." Pretending everything was going as planned was a lot like lying and made him sick to his stomach. But for now he had no choice.

"How long did you say Hester has been the bookkeeper here?"

"She's been with Peter from the beginning."

Diana had heard the story about why Hester was leaving from her mother, who'd heard it from Cheryl, who'd most likely heard it from Andrew, who'd heard it from Peter. She liked getting her information a little closer to the source. "And why is she leaving now?"

He reached behind her and turned off the office light, then closed the door. "Her husband, David, died a couple of months ago after a long god-awful battle with cancer. He went through chemo and radiation—and everything else mainstream medicine could do for him—and he wasn't in remission six months before the cancer showed up again.

"Hester couldn't deal with the suggestion by David's doctors that he begin hospice. Which made her an easy target when a woman came into the gallery to buy prints for an alternative medicine cancer clinic she and her husband had opened in Big Sur. The woman got Hester to tell her about David and what he was going through. One thing led to another, and by the time the woman left the gallery, she'd convinced Hester they could cure David no matter how far his cancer had spread, completely contradicting what David's oncologists had told them."

"The same kind of thing happened to my uncle and his wife," Diana said. "The family tried to tell them they were being scammed, but who are you going to believe when you're being bombarded with a parade of people coming to your house telling you about their miracle cures?"

"Her friends did some investigating and discovered the doctor had closed his first clinic under a cloud of ongoing charges of health care fraud. Hester's way of dealing with that kind of information was to stop seeing her friends."

Michael led Diana into the main part of the gallery. "When David died last Christmas, she fell apart. It was like she was trying to climb a greased pole to get out of her depression. She got into the habit of staying up all night and not coming to work until one or two o'clock in the afternoon. Then, because she was falling behind on her work, she would stay until midnight. She stunned everyone when she put up her house for sale, and told Peter that as soon as she took care of some unfinished business, she was moving to Oregon to be with her sister."

They wandered from room to room, Diana stopping to stare at prints that caught her eye, Michael telling her behind-the-picture stories. The majority were ocean scenes, but several of her favorites were portrayals of day-to-day life along the coast, the subjects surprisingly eclectic, going from sheep grazing in the shade of an old barn to monarch butterflies wintering over in a grove of pine trees. There were portraits, too, almost all of them showing the subject in contemplation. The work was sentimental but not mawkish, the kind of art that broke through a snarky critic's opinion to grace the walls of cottages and corporate offices alike, because it spoke to the person who loved it.

In the last room on the main floor, tucked between a picture of a robin stretching to capture a red berry and one with a couple walking hand in hand on a moonlit beach, was a portrait that struck her with such force she couldn't stop staring. The image was simple, a young girl sitting on a fog-shrouded beach, her back to the artist, her chestnut hair blowing gently in a breeze, her arm draped lovingly around a dog that leaned tightly into her side.

"Recognize her?" Michael said.

Diana frowned. "The girl?"

"The dog."

She looked closer. "Is that Coconut?"

He nodded. "In one of her few quiet moments when she was a puppy."

"Then the girl must be Shiloh."

"It was her first day back after three weeks in the hospital. She desperately wanted to spend it at the beach, but Jeremy had arranged for a visiting nurse to stay with her at home. He had a meeting that he either attended or lost a job that was in the bid process. Peter happened to overhear what was going on and offered to spend the afternoon with Shiloh—if she would sit for him. She knew she was being manipulated and that sitting for Peter was more a way to keep her from overextending herself, but she also knew it was the only way she was going to get what she wanted.

"While she tried to see the humpbacks that had been reported in the area through the fog, he sketched. This was the result of that day."

"I love that story," Diana said. "And I love the way I feel when I look at the picture. Even though you can't see her face you can tell how special that moment was and how much it meant for her to be there."

"I've known a lot of people who feel they're coming home when they're at the ocean, but none like Shiloh. My mom told her she must have been a mermaid in another life."

Diana had never known a guy her own age like Michael and wasn't sure how to respond to him. His kindness was real. And natural. As much a part of him as his lopsided smile. She could picture him turning down a date with Taylor Swift if Shiloh or his mother or Jeremy or Peter or anyone he knew needed him. What kind of twenty-nine-year-old man was like that? And why? "She sounds like a special little girl."

"Not so little anymore. She'll be twelve in a couple of months."

"I'm looking forward to meeting her."

Michael stared at her through narrowed eyes for what seemed like a long time before saying anything. "She'll like you."

Diana dipped her chin to hide the flush of pleasure that swept her cheeks. She was used to guys saying nice things about her hair or her eyes or her body, but never about who she was inside.

"Is the original painting available?" she asked, suspecting a Peter Wylie original would cost what her house would cost. If she still had a house.

"If it were, I could have sold it a hundred times." Michael reached out to tap the right-hand corner of the frame to straighten the infinitesimally crooked print. "Peter gave it to Shiloh."

They'd talked about Jeremy and Shiloh during lunch, too, so Diana knew the basics. Still she sensed there had been a lot left unsaid. She'd been filled with curiosity, but didn't push for answers. It was obvious Michael felt protective of his friends.

She moved to the final wall of pictures in what logically would have been the living room before the house was converted.

"Why two galleries?" she asked, standing in front of a picture of a sea otter.

"The Carmel gallery was too small to handle originals and prints. Peter considered moving up the coast to Half Moon Bay, but it was too far away for him to spend more than a day or two a month up there. He likes to meet the people who buy his pictures. Personal contact is important to the way he does business."

"I think it's great that you wound up working with him. Having the two of you hit it off must have felt like a great gift to your mom."

"It was hard in the beginning," he admitted. "Especially when my dad wanted to get back together with my mom, and it seemed to me and my brother that Peter was the only thing keeping them apart. But then I saw it for what it was, and instead of getting sucked into taking sides, Paul and I got out of the way so they could work it out themselves. Julia was a big help."

"Girlfriend?"

"Julia?" He laughed. "Not even close. Not only is she married to a best-selling writer, she has a houseful of kids and lives three thousand miles away."

The name connected. "She's the owner of the beach house that Jeremy is working on."

"She insists she's its caretaker, that the real owners were and always will be a couple named Joe and Maggie."

"That's the way I felt about the house my great-grandfather built. He and my great-grandmother willed it to my grandmother and then when she died, I bought it from the estate. I considered myself the caretaker for the next generation."

"It must be great to feel that kind of connection."

"Yeah," she said softly. "It did."

Michael came to a set of stairs. "There's a one bedroom apartment on the second floor with a great view of the boardwalk. It's where I used to stay when I came home from college during summer breaks. Living so close made it convenient to learn the business. Of course I didn't have a clue that it was a setup. I was being groomed to take over running the galleries when Peter and my mother toured Europe every other summer."

Before she thought how it would sound, she blurted out, "So, working here during the summer is all you do?"

Michael laughed. "That, and getting my PhD, and traveling, and substitute teaching for a couple of years, and writing environmental blogs for several—"

She held up her hands in surrender. "Any more and I'm going to feel like a slacker."

She looked to the top of the staircase. "Is this how you get to the lighthouse part?"

"There's another set of stairs off the kitchen that takes you up there."

"Can I see?"

"Sure—but it can get claustrophobic."

"I don't mind. I was stuck inside a paper-mache cow for four hours and did okay."

"You don't expect me to let that one go."

She pulled the elastic band from her hair and shook her head. "I was in Future Farmers of America in high school and we made an overly ambitious float for the Fourth of July parade. The cow was supposed to be animated, but the motor stopped running just as we pulled into line. Which meant we either settled for second place—*again*—or put someone inside to manipulate the head and tail by hand. That someone turned out to be me."

"The parade lasted four hours?" Michael had an insane urge to touch her hair to see if it really was as soft and silky as it looked.

"Oh, there's more." She grinned. "The hole I crawled through wouldn't stay closed so someone came up with the brilliant idea to use superglue. Of course all this happened before they told us that an alarm had gone off at a bank on the parade route and we wouldn't be allowed to start until they made sure it was safe.

"So, I either stayed inside the cow or they cut a hole in its belly. Which meant we would have a mutilated nonfunctioning animated cow as the main feature on our float. This was the first time in three years that we actually had a chance at first place. You can understand why no one was anxious to cut me out."

Michael showed her the apartment and it was everything she could do to keep from asking about the rent, knowing there was no way she could afford it. Not only was the apartment the perfect size, it was fully furnished and decorated in all her favorite colors.

They left the apartment and went down the hallway to another locked door. This room held the circular steel stairway. Every riser creaked and groaned; the sides came in closer and closer as the tower narrowed. Finally, they reached the top.

Michael unlatched a window and swung it open before he moved aside so Diana could join him.

"Oh, wow," she said, leaning forward until she could see the entire coastline over the rooftops of the single-story homes between the gallery and the beach. Sailboats skimmed the sun-dappled water, a dozen surfers lazily rode their boards as they waited for a wave. "Wow, wow, wow. I'll bet you used to spend a lot of time up here. I know I would."

"It's even better at night, especially in winter when it's clear and there's a full moon and the air is crisp and cold. I used to imagine this was a real lighthouse on an isolated point of land and it was just me and the seagulls."

"I'm not sure I could do that—be a lighthouse keeper, I mean. I don't mind being alone, but not for more than a day or two at a time."

Michael spotted something to his left. "Look over here," he said, pointing.

"Give me a hint what I'm looking for."

"Just keep watching."

Nothing happened. "I don't see anything." And then she did. "Oh my God," she grabbed his arm. "Is that a whale?"

"It is."

"Why is she coming up out of the water like that?"

"It's called breaching, and she could either do it all day or come up one time and disappear." He'd forgotten how great it felt to share the excitement of someone discovering the magic of the ocean for the first time.

"This is just so friggin' cool."

He liked her enthusiasm almost as much as he liked that

she hadn't immediately let go of his arm. She was so close he could feel her warmth and smell a trace of lavender in her hair. A sobering thought threaded its way through his mind. The more confident he made her feel about fitting in, the harder it was going to be to tell her she didn't. "Once you've been here a while, you'll get used to it."

"No, I won't." And she wouldn't. This was too special.

"*There*—" He pointed again, only this time straight out in front of them.

She looked in time to see three whales breeching together and laughed in excitement. "I never, not in a million years, dreamed I would see something this special. Thank you so much for bringing me here."

It was impossible not to get caught up in her energy. "What else have you seen since you've been here?"

She looked at him. "I'm not sure I know what you mean."

"Otters? Dolphins? Pelicans?"

She shook her head. "I haven't seen anything, unless surfers count."

Michael glanced at his watch a second time and frowned.

"Your meeting—I forgot."

"I'm sorry," he said, meaning it more than he would have believed before he'd met her. "It's something I can't get out of."

She took one last look, as if snapping a mental photograph, then maneuvered herself into position to climb downstairs. "Thank you," she said again when they were back in the main part of the gallery.

"All part of the new employee package." He cringed. Could he sound more inane? Michael set the alarm and locked the back door. He paused to watch her cross to the car before he stepped off the porch and followed, recognizing the hole in the sand he'd dug with what he'd told her that day, and knowing the deeper it went, the more disastrous it would be when the sides caved in.

Chapter Six

· · · · · · · · · ·

"I DON'T WANT to lose Diana," Peter said. "There has to be a way we can handle this without involving her."

"I'm listening," Michael said. He didn't want to lose her either, and not just for the obvious reasons.

"I don't want you to *listen,* I want you to figure it out." Frustration, as alien to his personality as pessimism, permeated Peter's words.

Michael shifted the phone to his other ear as he crossed the living room. In the lengthy process of becoming more friends than relatives, he and Peter had reached the point that they never minced words with each other. "We're in over our heads, Peter. We don't have a clue what we're doing."

"Tell me again what happened that made you suspicious."

"How many times—"

"Indulge me. This is how I work things out."

Michael tolerated Peter's request because he understood

where it was coming from. Peter no more wanted to believe Hester had been stealing from the business than Michael did. Maybe there was something they'd failed to see, something that could provide another explanation for all that missing money.

"When the owner of West Bay Images called last week, he said he couldn't get Hester to return his calls or answer his emails. He told me they hadn't been paid in three months, and that they wouldn't ship the new prints we'd ordered until we made a good-faith payment on the current bill."

Peter let out a barely audible groan. "He must think we're on the verge of bankruptcy. Jesus, that kind of rumor could destroy both me and the business."

"Do you want me to finish, or have you heard enough?" Michael asked.

"What I really want is for you to tell me how the hell I could have missed something so obvious."

"You didn't see it because you didn't want to." He could have added, and probably should have, that Peter was not only too trusting, he was a lousy businessman. Michael would bet six months salary that Peter hadn't looked at the books in months, if not years. He signed whatever Hester put in front of him, no questions asked.

"I can't stop thinking about Hester taking the money. Why would she do something like that? Why didn't she just come to me if she needed something?"

"Maybe she was afraid you would try to talk her out of paying for all those treatments for David."

"That doesn't make sense. She had insurance. Everyone

who works at the galleries has top-notch insurance—the best my broker could find for them."

"Doesn't matter. No insurance company will cover treatment at a non-accredited facility."

"What are you talking about?"

"I did some snooping around last week and discovered that neither the doctor nor the hospital where David was treated were legit. You needed a magnifying glass to read the disclaimer, but it was there."

Peter groaned. "And that's where the money went? To some scam artist?"

"I don't know that for a fact, but I think it's a damn good guess."

"So how do I clean up this mess? Where do we stand with West Bay Images?"

Michael sat on the edge of the sofa and leaned forward to prop his elbows on his knees. "I apologized about the bill, paid it with the business credit card, and spent the next twenty minutes reassuring him that it was a fluke that would never happen again. Even after all of that, he still switched us to a pay-as-you-go account for the rest of the year."

"That son of a bitch—half his business has come from people I sent to him, and he has the balls to do something like this." Realizing he was shouting, he lowered his voice. "And then as soon as you hung up, you tried to reach Hester."

"Several times. I called and texted and sent emails. Nothing. The only time I hear from her is when she leaves a message on the phone at the gallery saying she isn't feeling well and won't be in."

"You've gone to her house?"

"Three times," Michael said patiently. "She's not there."

"Could she be hiding?"

"Are you listening to how bizarre this sounds? Why would she be hiding in her own house?"

"Why won't she answer her goddamned phone?" Peter shouted.

Michael didn't bother answering the rhetorical question. "What made you decide to go through the files rather than wait to ask her what was going on?"

"The guy at West Bay was such a jerk, I wanted to find something that would prove he'd been paid and that the error was on his end. All I needed was a bank statement showing—"

Peter let out a heavy sigh. "You don't have to go on. When was the last time you tried calling Hester?"

Michael glanced at his watch. "Twenty-five minutes ago." Consumed with frustration over not being able to do anything to help, Michael said, "I'm going to make an appointment with your attorney tomorrow."

"You're wasting your time, Michael. She's going to tell you she's not a criminal attorney, and that you're going to have to find someone else to represent the galleries in this."

"We don't need her to represent us," Michael said, struggling for patience. "We need advice. If she doesn't have the answers, she has to know someone who would."

"All right, say she does. And let's say you make an appointment with him or her and they tell you that you have to turn everything over to the police. What then? If you don't, you become complicit. If you do, Hester winds up in jail."

"We're right back where we started. Without talking to Hester or getting someone to go over the books, we're only guessing at what's going on."

"It can't be Diana," Peter insisted. "I will not let her become involved in this."

"Then who?"

"I don't know. I'll figure it out when I get there."

"And in the meantime? What do I tell Diana? What possible excuse can I give her to keep her from showing up for work on Monday?"

"Once this is settled and she knows that asking her to wait a couple of weeks had nothing to do with her, that we were only trying to protect her, she'll understand."

"By the time that happens, she's going to be long gone," Michael said.

"Do you have a better suggestion?"

An idea hit with surprising clarity. "Up her stake in staying. Offer her the apartment."

Several seconds passed before Peter replied. "What makes you think that will work?"

"She's seen it and she loves it. And she'll know you would never make that kind of offer if you wanted to get rid of her."

"I hope you're right. Do you want me to handle it when I get there?" Peter said.

"I think it would be better coming from you."

"So what about the attorney?"

Michael yielded. "As long as we've got Diana taken care

of, I'm willing to wait for that, too. In the meantime I'll do whatever it takes to make sure she knows you're glad she's here, and that you're looking forward to working with her."

Peter chuckled. "From what I've heard, that shouldn't be an onerous burden."

Michael ignored him. "Back to the attorney. You need to be putting some thought into what you're going to do if she says you have to turn this over to the police."

"That's not going to happen. She'll be working for me, what I tell her will be covered under attorney-client privilege and won't go any further—not even if I tell her there was a crime committed."

"Are you sure about that?"

"Yes." A second later he added, "No. How the hell would I know something like that for sure?"

"Where did you hear it?" The only time Peter ever got short-tempered with him was when he was unsure of his position. To have it happen now wasn't a good sign.

Several seconds passed. "On some television show. It made sense, so I figured they must know what they were talking about. After all, they have a staff of advisors working for them."

Michael laughed out loud. This was the Peter he knew, someone who could poke fun at himself and get a kick out of doing so. "Please tell me it wasn't daytime television."

"It was one of those lawyer shows your mom likes."

"Does she know you're planning to base Hester's legal defense on *The Good Wife*?"

"No. And don't you dare tell her."

"What's it worth to you?"

Now it was Peter's turn to laugh. "Name your price."

"A confirmed meeting with your attorney when you get home."

"All right. I'll call her first thing in the morning to set it up."

"When are you getting in?"

"The first flight we could manage without a long layover leaves four hours after the reception in Brussels. We get in around noon, and should be home by three."

The Brussels reception brought in dealers from all over northern Europe, and provided a sizable percentage of Peter's foreign income. It couldn't be missed. Which meant they wouldn't be home for five days.

A lot could happen in five days.

"I'll see you then," Michael said.

"Before you hang up, I want to tell you again how sorry I am that you're caught up in this."

"Get over it, Peter. We're going to figure it out." Michael stopped pacing, hiked himself up to sit on the island counter, and grabbed an orange out of the mesh basket beside him. He'd spent hours on the Internet looking for an answer that would keep all of them out of court. What he'd found were articles written with conviction, immediately followed by equivocation, advice as helpful as a rubber life raft with a hole in it.

"If it turns out Hester did take the money, she had a damn good reason." Pain edged the words like frost forming on ice. "I want to hear her side before I do something I'm going to regret later."

"I understand." There was nothing more to say. Michael dug a thumb-sized opening into the orange peel. He had to wait for what came next.

"And I'm sorry that it's falling on you to try to keep Diana from leaving."

Michael smiled as he added another quarter-size piece of peel to the growing stack. "Don't worry about it."

Chapter Seven

· · · · · · · · · ·

MICHAEL HUNG UP from his conversation with Peter and hit contacts on his phone, looking for Diana's number. She answered on the second ring. "Are you free tonight?"

"Michael?"

"Yeah—sorry. I should have identified myself."

Assuming he wanted to show her the Carmel gallery to finish the tour, she answered with a breezy, "Sure. What did you have in mind?"

"Dinner. There's a wonderful hole-in-the-wall Mexican restaurant near the wharf that's great for watching surfers and sunsets. I'm not sure where it's written, but everyone out here knows that there's no way you can be a true Californian and not love authentic Mexican food."

To anyone listening it would sound as if he were asking her on a date. But Diana knew better. She recognized the subtle pressure that had been exerted on Michael by Cheryl. As the baby of her generation in their far-reaching

amily, it was the duty of her elders to make sure she was
aken care of.

"It's not as if we don't have Mexican food in Topeka."
before he could say anything, she added, "And, yes, I do real-
ze Taco Bell doesn't count as real Mexican food."

"The thought never crossed my mind."

"You don't lie very well."

"Some people think that's a good thing."

She laughed. "I see your point."

"Are we on?" he asked.

"Yes. What time?"

"Pick you up at five-thirty?"

It wasn't as if she had anything else to do. "I'll be ready."

MICHAEL'S WHITE PRIUS pulled into the driveway at five
wenty-nine. Diana grabbed a quick look at her reflection in
he living room window, smoothing the skirt of the blue and
uchsia sundress she'd brought with her from Kansas, hoping
he skinny straps and above-the-knee hemline would make
er look like she belonged.

Michael got out of the car to greet her. "Great dress."

"Thanks."

They took the back roads to the restaurant, avoiding
he traffic on Highway 1. Everywhere she looked there were
eople walking or running or strolling hand in hand. Dogs
ccompanied half of them, some riding in their own strollers.

Dinner was everything Michael had promised, includ-
ng the sunset. He'd ordered a sampler appetizer that had

a variety of ten different foods served at the restaurant. She readily admitted she'd never heard of half of the offerings. Afterward, Michael asked her to list her favorites. It turned out to be the hardest thing she'd done that day. She settled on her top three—beef birria, arroz con camarones, and halibut ceviche.

Instead of heading to the car when they left the restaurant, Michael took her to the marina, where they sat on a rock wall and watched the boats come in. Seagulls swooped in to check for remnants of fish and any other discarded bits of food left behind. A pelican stood guard atop a schooner mast.

"Do you have a boat?" she asked.

"I have friends who've taught me to sail, but I've never had the desire to go out on my own."

"It must be mind-blowing to be out on the ocean with whales and dolphins all around you. Just sitting here looking at the boats is special." She had almost added—*with you*— but caught herself in time.

"It looks peaceful now," he said. "But you should have seen it four years ago when the tsunami that hit Japan made it over here. The waves weren't impressive as they were coming in, but they caused millions of dollars in damages when they swept into the harbor. Boats and docks and pillars were stacked on top of each other like they'd been tossed in a toy chest by a kid throwing a tantrum."

She tried to imagine what it had been like, but couldn't picture what Michael had seen. Now it was like going into a town hit by a tornado after the debris had been hauled away.

"Thank you," Diana said, deciding not to wait until the

evening was over. "Today was everything I hoped it would be when Cheryl told me about the job at the gallery."

"You're welcome. I'm glad you had a good time." From the beginning she'd been easy to be with, their words unguarded and conversations free-flowing. She'd laughed at his jokes because she thought they were funny, not out of politeness. And she was game for anything, including, despite his warning, a serrano pepper that she unceremoniously spit into her napkin.

"Are you dating anyone?" Diana asked impulsively.

He looked down and nudged an empty shell with his foot, trying to hide the grin of pleasure that came with her question. She'd tried to make it sound casual, but no one asked something like that unless they were interested in the answer.

"Nope. I've given up on anything permanent. For now, at least." He focused on a wooden skiff making the turn into the harbor. "At least that was how I felt when I got up this morning."

"Me, too." She shot him a glance to make sure he meant what he'd said. "The last thing I want is to get involved in another relationship. At least not right away. Not after the last one." She was babbling.

"That's how I felt when Leslie and I broke up. It's been almost a year. Actually more like nine months, two weeks, and fourteen hours. But I'm over it now."

"Sorry." She loved his quirky sense of humor. "I didn't mean to bring it all back."

He picked up the shell and tossed it in the water, drawing the attention of several nearby gulls. "I'm kidding about the time. And don't be sorry, there's not a whole lot you could have done to change what happened, unless you're really good at talking people out of making asses of themselves."

Because she'd never been able to let go of anything, she did exactly what the reasonable side of her brain told her not to and asked, "So, what happened?"

He cast her a sideways glance and a halfhearted attempt at a grin. "I'll tell you about it in the car."

On the way to the parking lot Michael pointed out landmarks and cormorants and talked about the locations Peter had painted. Although he'd never thought of himself as a tour guide, he discovered, to his surprise, that he liked showing her his California.

When they were in the car, he picked up where he'd left off earlier. "I proposed to her."

Diana ran through a dozen reasons she and her girlfriends had used to dump a guy, and being proposed to had never made any of their lists. "That's it?"

"If only." He buckled his seat belt, put in an odd looking key, and hit an ignition button.

"I don't know whether you want me to shut up or drag it out of you."

"Instead of a quiet romantic dinner at a five-star restaurant, I asked her to marry me at AT&T Park during a Giants baseball game."

"That's it?"

"—on the Jumbotron."

"Oh . . ."

"Exactly." A car slowed and waved him in. Michael

nodded his thanks and eased between a green BMW and a white pickup truck.

"She wasn't ready, I take it."

"Not even close. I'd misread every signal she'd given me about romantic proposals."

Diana frowned. "Somehow I don't see you as the kind of guy who would do something like the proposal you described."

"Thanks. I'm glad that comes across."

"Then why?"

"When we first started going together, Leslie told me she loved that kind of wildly romantic gesture. She even took me to a theater where a guy had made one of those ads you see before the movie starts, only instead of pushing dental implants, he was pushing himself and all the reasons his girlfriend should marry him."

"Oh, how painful. So what did Leslie do when you proposed?"

"Well, after I went down on bended knee and told her she was the love of my life and that I wanted to grow old with her, she took one look at the ring, clasped her hands behind her back, and said she wanted to kill me. She was in the middle of telling me how furious she was that I would embarrass her in front of our friends, all of whom I'd made sure were there, when she realized it wasn't just our friends who were watching."

Diana groaned in sympathy.

"If only it had been that simple," Michael said, "she might have forgiven me. But once she heard the collection of gasps and hoots from what was an estimated crowd of twenty thousand people and figured out what I'd done, all hope I had that eventually she would come around disappeared. Thankfully whoever was running the camera cut away before she burst into tears and took off."

There wasn't one guy in Diana's circle of friends who would dream of doing something as wildly romantic, let alone own it after it fell apart. What was even harder to imagine was any of them having empathy for the girl who'd turned them down.

Feeling like a hypocrite, Diana repeated her mother's favorite platitude. "Give it some time. It'll get easier."

"Really? That's the best you can do?" The playfully mocking tone took the edge off the question.

Diana laughed. "Pretty lame, huh?"

"Worse—it's actually true," he admitted. "It took six months, but I finally reached the point that I could watch a Giants game for more than five minutes and be able to tell you what happened on the field."

"And now?"

"I can get through an entire inning, no problem. A friend of mine recently gave me a couple of tickets for their next home game that I'm going to use. Not in the same section, but close enough."

"Good for you." Gathering the weight of the idiotic thing she'd done on one side of a scale, and Michael's screwy miscalculation on the other, her side came in several pounds heavier. She needed more time to get where he was now. Still he gave her hope.

"Want to go with me?"

It was obvious by the way he asked that the invitation wasn't planned. "Who are they playing?"

"Does it matter?"

Her eyes widened in surprise. "Of course it does. I might have to cheer for the Giants if they were playing a team I don't like."

Michael laughed. "Good answer. I'll check the tickets and get back to you."

Chapter Eight

· · · · · · · · · ·

IT WAS NEAR midnight when Michael dropped off Diana at the cottage. Even though she was still operating on Kansas time, and should have been wrung out, she wasn't ready for the night to end. Plus, she didn't have to go to work in the morning. She had four more days she could sleep in as late as she wanted.

She reached for the door handle. "It's been a great day. The best I've had in a long time. Thank you."

"You're welcome. I had a good time, too."

She got out of the car and leaned down to say one last thing before going inside. "Would it be all right if I stopped by the Carmel gallery tomorrow?"

No, it was not all right. "Friday would be better. It's slower then."

Obviously disappointed, she shrugged and said, "Okay."

"Come around noon." He could handle this. He'd give her a quick tour, and then take her to lunch. "There's a great pub on Ocean Avenue where they—"

"Only if you let me buy," she insisted.

"This particular pub gives me a great discount."

The one thing he could have said to make her rethink her decision. "Really?"

"Sometimes," he admitted. "It depends on who's working that day."

She smiled. He was so easy. "See you tomorrow night."

He waited until she was at the door before he backed out of the driveway. Diana waved and stepped inside, dropped her purse on the entry table, and went into the bedroom to change into jeans and a lightweight sweatshirt. She put on a pair of flip-flops, then stepped out of them. Where she was going she didn't need shoes.

Minutes later she opened the door and saw Michael leaning against the fender of his car, his arms folded across his chest, his lips curved into a crooked grin.

"You're fast," he said.

"What are you doing here?"

"It seemed like a good night for a walk on the beach."

She moved to join him. "How did you know?"

"Just a hunch." He held out his hand. "Shall we go?"

Again with the hand-holding. Was this something everyone did in California, or was it unique to Michael? Not that she minded. Actually, she kind of liked it. Probably because she didn't sense he was doing it for any other reason than he liked it, too.

When they reached the wooden stairway to the beach, Michael sat down to take off his tennis shoes and put them next to a patch of maiden grass. Instead of waiting for him to get up again, Diana plopped down beside him, pulling up her legs and propping her chin on her knees.

A full moon dominated the sky, laying a silver pathway across a surprisingly still ocean. A slowly encroaching high tide nudged the shoreline, the waves playing with a piece of driftwood and washing away the remnants of a sand castle built too close to the water.

"I won't," she said.

"Okay . . ." he replied slowly, doing a quick mental search to try to figure out what she was talking about. Giving up, he scooped a handful of sand and let it sift through his fingers while he waited for her to go on.

She turned to him and smiled. "I won't ever get used to this. I don't see how anyone could."

"Are you talking about me personally, or people in general?"

"You?"

"Never gonna happen," he said.

"I didn't think so." She turned to look at him.

"Cheryl said you were looking to make the move out here permanent." There were other bookkeeping jobs Peter could help her find. She wouldn't have to go back to Kansas, if she didn't want to. "Of course, that was when she was deep into the sales pitch about why Peter should hire you."

"She wasn't misleading you. I love Kansas, but something happened that stole my sense of belonging."

"It must have been pretty bad."

She didn't like putting her feelings into words. But there was something about him listening to what she would say that made them tumble out like coins from a winning slot machine. "I stopped believing in myself. I was willing to settle for whatever came my way because I was so desperate to be like all my friends. It was the only way I knew to fit in."

"I get that. But something awful had to happen to push you off the cliff."

"Would you be surprised if I told you it was a guy?"

"No more than you were surprised when I told you I made an ass out of myself because of a girl. We're human. It's the kind of thing we do." He plucked a piece of the tall grass and pulled the seed end through his pinched fingers. "It's not fair for me to put this off on Leslie. I should have realized what she saw as romantic for someone else didn't necessarily translate into something she wanted for herself. She had nothing to do with what I did."

"She must have given off some kind of signal that she was in love with you. Maybe not on-bended-knee-in-front-of-twenty-thousand-people love, but *something*."

"There was never any doubt that we were in love, at least in the beginning. She'd even jokingly proposed to me when we were in Hawaii, and everyone thought we were on our honeymoon. Hell, when her sister had a baby, Leslie started talking about what she wanted to name our firstborn. What I didn't recognize was what was real between us and what was role-playing. She loved the idea of being in love more than she loved me."

"Do you still love her?"

He shook his head. "We almost made it to being friends when she met the guy she's with now. He wasn't comfortable having me around. So that was it." Tossing the seeds into the air, he put his hands on the wooden plank and stood. "Let's see what treasures the tide brought in."

She followed him down the stairs. "I saw an old couple swinging a wand across the sand this morning. Is that what they were doing? Looking for treasure?"

"Mary and Harold have been combing this beach with their metal detectors for as long as my family has been coming here. They own the white house on the other side of the cove. When my brother Paul and I were kids, Harold convinced us that he and Mary made so much money with the things they found that they didn't have to work a regular job."

"Not true, I take it."

"About as far away from the truth as Lance Armstrong swearing he never took drugs. I was in my high school computer science class when I came across their names as co-inventors of one of the first microchips that increased layers without increasing size. What they did led to the microchip we have now that's the size of a dot. I looked them up and discovered they were on the Forbes list of the country's billionaires. Although last I heard they'd given the majority of it away."

"I'd like to do that one day." She stopped to pick up an almost perfectly round, flattened shell. "Of course before I can give money away, I have to figure out how to make it."

"You don't need a lot to give away some."

She looked at him to see if he was serious. "You do that?"

"Yeah, of course. It's no big deal."

She didn't know one person near her own age who didn't

think buying Girl Scout cookies was a major charitable contribution. "Any charity in particular?"

He seemed uncomfortable at the question, and for a minute Diana thought he was going to brush it off. "Lupus Foundation and Make a Wish," he finally said.

When was she going to learn to keep her mouth shut and not pry into people's private lives? "I'm sorry. That was none of my business."

"Ask me whatever you want."

"I'm assuming you're involved in those two particular charities because it's personal?"

It was, but he answered anyway. "I know there's no way they're going to come up with a cure in time for Shiloh, but I'd like to think one day there'll be a child who doesn't have to face what she does."

"I don't know anything about lupus."

"It's an autoimmune disease that doesn't follow a set course. It can show up in a dozen different ways, from rashes to kidney failure to heart disease to joint pain."

"How long have you known Jeremy and Shiloh?"

"Jeremy and I go back to my freshman year in college when Peter hired him to add another bedroom to his house. Paul, my brother, and I needed a place to stay when we were here. Jeremy and his wife had adopted Shiloh as an infant and by the time she was two, they were deep into dealing with her lupus. The next summer he hired me to do the scut work that came with rebuilding a house that had structural damage from one of our smaller earthquakes. I worked for him three summers, and to supplement the poverty wages he paid, he taught me the difference between being a craftsman who builds solid wood cabinets from scratch and one who installs factory-made MDF laminate."

"My great-grandfather was a craftsman. He hand made every door and staircase and piece of furniture in the house he built for my great-grandmother." And now, thanks to her, it was all gone, even the furniture.

Diana stopped to pick up another shell, feeling a shiver of excitement at the idea that she was actually doing something she'd spent her childhood dreaming about. Until she'd pulled into the driveway and stepped out of her ten-year-old Camry, she'd never truly believed she would ever leave Kansas. And here she was—walking on a beach with the Pacific Ocean stretching out before her like a magical blue carpet.

"It's a sand dollar," Michael said when she held out the shell to him. "When they're alive they're covered by small hairs that help them move across the ocean floor." He held the sand dollar tilted to the moonlight to show her the pattern on the shell.

"That's so pretty," she said. "It's like a flower. Would it be okay if I kept it? It's not against the law or anything, is it?"

Michael laughed. "The first kid who finds it in the morning will step on it just to hear the crunch. It's almost as satisfying as popping seaweed pods."

"Or bubble wrap?"

"Oh, no—you're not one of those," he said with teasing distain.

"Compulsively so."

He found another sand dollar and handed it to her. "For your collection."

She tucked them in her sweatshirt pocket and paused a minute to watch Michael as he searched the shoreline for more shells. When he stopped to see why she wasn't following, he flashed a smile that almost made her gasp. Smiles from men who looked like Michael were supposed to be slightly surly, a bad-boy kind of thing, like the one James Dean had in the poster her sister put up when she was ten and didn't take down until the day she married a guy who was more Logan Lerman than James Dean.

"I'm coming," she said. She spotted a wave that was headed straight toward her, its force stronger than any of the others she'd already dodged. Instead of backing up, she went toward it, letting the edge of the wave wash over her feet and climb her ankles.

"Holy crap," she said loud enough to disturb the seagulls halfway to the cliff. "I thought it was going to be warm." Still, she didn't move. How could she? This, too, was part of her dream.

Michael held out his hand. "Come up here where it's still warm and dig your feet into the sand."

She took his hand and let him lead her to the remnant of what must have been a magnificent tree a long, long time ago. The trunk, a weathered gray, lay on the ground, the top and sides as smooth as if it had been sanded and polished.

"This is what passes for a bench on our little beach," he said. "It's a great place to come when you have to work something out or when you just want to be alone."

She sat on the end where there were still cut marks from a logger's saw. Putting her legs out in front of her and crossing her ankles, she adjusted her sweatshirt to protect her shells. "How did it get here?"

Instead of sitting next to Diana, Michael settled on the sand and used the log for a backrest. "It was brought in during a storm back in the seventies. A log this size is fairly rare this far south, but common in Oregon. The people who were here when the storm came through say the surges were so powerful, they stripped half the sand from the cove and hauled it out to sea. It took more than two years, and help from the state, for the sand to return. By then another storm had pushed up the log even higher. For years a group of homeowners tried to get the state to use one of their bulldozers to push the log higher still, but it never happened." He spread both arms along the length of the log, put his head back and grinned.

"And then along came Tony Gallardo and his buddies."

She recognized the name but it took several seconds for it to register. "The movie star Tony Gallardo?"

Michael nodded. "He was filming a movie in Watsonville. By the time he and his buddies got off work, the beach was filled with people and there wasn't any place to set up a volleyball net. Then one night, without thinking anyone could or would be upset, they moved the log to clear a space. Luckily they moved the log up the beach, and not down."

She stared at the waves as she listened to Michael, counting them to see if every seventh one really was bigger than the rest. She was disappointed when it wasn't and started to urn away, when what looked like an innocent gentle wave hit vith a force that carried it twice as far as any that had gone pefore. "I'm going to like it here."

"What brought that on?"

"Some things you just know."

"What if I told you that Tony doesn't live here anymore? He sold the house on the cliff he used to own to Chris Sadler."

She laughed. "Well, that changes everything. Looks like 'll be headed back to corn country as soon as you can find omeone to take my place at the galleries." She focused on vhat he'd just told her. "Wait a minute. Are you talking bout the Chris Sadler who just won an Oscar?"

"That's him."

"Damn—looks like I'm going to have to reconsider eaving."

"Whatever it takes to keep you here." One way or another e was going to find a way to make this work.

"What about Peter—and your mom. Don't they get a ote?"

"Minor details." He picked up a broken shell and tossed t toward the ocean. She needed as much honesty as he could give her. "You have the personality and enthusiasm we need t the galleries right now. This has been a difficult year for Hester. She's had a hard time holding it together for the past ouple of years. Sometimes it comes out in her dealings with he customers, but most often it's our vendors that bear the prunt."

He picked up another shell and tossed it toward the

first. "Forget I said that. None of this involves you or is your problem."

"It's helpful to know what I'm walking into. Is there any thing I can do to make the transition easier? Would it help if I came in a couple of days early and let Hester go over the accounts with me?"

He felt like the guy who'd painted himself into a corner with slow-drying varnish.

"I'm not sure anything would help at this point," he said. "Leaving was Hester's idea, not Peter's."

"It's a lot easier to leave because you want to instead of going into your boss's office expecting a raise and walking out unemployed." She shifted so that she was sitting on the sand beside him, her back to the log.

"Is that what happened to you?"

"I thought you knew what happened." For awhile, between her mother and father, her brothers and sisters, the firefighters who'd watched her grandmother's house burn to the ground, and most of all Howard, she'd been convinced there were enough sources that the gossip had reached Outer Mongolia.

"By the time the story got to me it had gone through so many tellings, the only thing I paid attention to was that a really good bookkeeper needed a job, and Peter needed a really good bookkeeper. Serendipity."

"I love that word."

"Bookkeeper?"

She playfully punched him on his arm, hitting muscle that was rock hard. It was nice having a guy like Michael a a new friend, someone who either didn't know or didn't care how deeply she'd humiliated herself, and how profound the consequences had been. She didn't want to go there anymore than she wanted to tell Michael something that would make him doubt Peter's decision to hire her.

Still . . .

Chapter Nine

· · · · · · · · ·

DIANA BROUGHT UP her legs and wrapped her arms around them, careful not to disturb the delicate shells in her pocket. Staring at the ocean with the realization that what she could see was only a tiny fraction of what was out there helped put what had happened to her into perspective. She was one person in a world of seven billion. Her story was insignificant compared to that of a woman who had to battle crocodiles every day to get drinking water for her family.

She took a deep breath and began.

"The day after I graduated from the University of Kansas, I went to work for WKB Industries in their accounting division. Back then it was one of the hottest companies on the Dow Jones, and I was convinced they were a great fit for the way I imagined my career going—two years to get myself established in a job, night school to study for my CPA license, steadily accruing benefits, Florida vacations in the winter; all in all, a solid upper middle class life. WKB was known for promoting from within, which meant that with normal attrition, there would be an opportunity for me to move up as soon as I was licensed."

She paused and watched the waves, thinking how boring her life must sound to someone like Michael. But it was what it was. Trying to make it sound better or more glamorous would make as much sense as Donald Trump's comb-over. "I saw myself retiring from WKB. I'd have a nice income from the stock-sharing program and I'd finally be able to travel.

"I was twenty-two at the time. Can you imagine? How does anyone that age actually plan to spend a lifetime behind a desk, when there are so many places to go and see in a world filled with all those billions of people? That's my sister. It isn't me." More out of nervousness than need, with only a light breeze coming off the ocean, Diana reached up to twist her hair into a coil and lay it across her shoulder.

"It isn't me, either," he said. "I've been lucky to have backpacked through Europe and New Zealand, but I've never seen the Great Wall or the Barrier Reef or the Ganges River." He twisted to face her. "Did you know there's a river dolphin that lives in the Ganges? It's endangered and will likely disappear in a couple of decades. I want a chance to see one before they're gone. Maybe even try to do something to save them."

"I don't know if I could do that," she said. "It breaks my heart just thinking about it."

He smiled, purposely lightening the mood. "You could always visit one of the temples while I'm out on the river."

"I could do that," she said, playing along.

"Back to your story," he prompted.

"Are you sure you really want to hear this?"

"Positive. It's a mandatory part of the employment package."

Everything he said, every look he gave her, every smile that lit up his eyes, made her like him more. Yet, past experience told her that there had to be a downside. Every man she'd ever gone out with had a downside.

"I'd been working at WKB for seven years, when my boss told me he had something important that he wanted to talk to me about. He had his secretary set up an appointment for ten o'clock on a Friday morning.

"That should have been the first clue that I wasn't being given a promotion. Friday is the day they fire people at WKB, but never in the morning, always the afternoon, which lulled me into a fantasy of my own making. The Friday thing is such a cliché, but like all clichés, based in fact. Fire a person late in the day, send someone to watch them clean out their desk, then quietly and quickly escort them out of the building. It's an incredibly effective way to get rid of people, practiced by all kinds of businesses, big and small."

"Not to mention heartless."

"Thanks to my own naiveté, it turned out to be particularly cold in my case." She smiled again, surprising herself. It was the first time she'd been able to look at what happened without feeling utterly humiliated.

"I'd used the money I had tucked away for a down payment on a new car to buy a dynamite knockoff Stella McCartney suit and a pair of Manolo Blahnik heels. It was the best thing that came out of that day. And one of the few things from that time that I still own."

"Did you bring them with you?"

"I brought everything I own with me. It took me less than an hour to pack, and I had enough room left in the trunk of my car to bring Cheryl the dishes my mother promised to send her when my grandmother died."

"Sorry—but that's a little hard for me to imagine. I don't have sisters, but I have a mother."

"Wait for the rest, you'll understand." Not wanting to see the look on his face when she told him what she'd done, she stretched out her legs in front of her and leaned back her head to focus on the blanket of stars filling the sky. "It turned out I wasn't the only one being fired that day. The company had decided to outsource my entire department. I was invited to apply for a job with the accounting company they'd hired. Of course it would mean I had to relocate to Louisiana and that I'd be hired at entry-level wages with minimum benefits. But what the hell, a job is a job."

"I assume you told them what they could do with their offer?"

"Oh, trust me. I thought of some brilliant comebacks, but not until I was in the car headed home. All I could do when it happened was hold myself together. I knew that if I started crying, I wouldn't be able to stop. And if I started screaming, they'd have me hauled off." She smiled. "And if I started throwing things the way I wanted to, I'd never get another job. This was the guy I had to go to for a reference letter, which he not so subtly reminded me in the same breath he used to fire me."

"Sounds like it was all carefully planned."

"The human resources department at WKB is top-notch. I have no doubt they had every possibility covered."

He surprised her then by reaching for her hand. This was different than the other times he'd held her hand. Now it was purposefully comforting, the kind of gesture that came with the intimacy of a real friendship. She'd been wrapped in bear hugs that were less familiar than the way Michael touched her.

"Their loss is our gain. Although I have to admit I don't think any of us knew you were an actual CPA. You're way overqualified for this job."

She shook off his comment. "There's more that's less impressive. I'd promised Howard, the guy who'd sworn his undying love when he gave me a flashy engagement ring at Christmas—which, apropos of nothing, turned out to be a one-and-a-half carat CZ, not a diamond—that I'd call him as soon as I got out of the meeting so he knew what kind of plans to make for our big celebration. The bigger the promotion, the more expensive the champagne. I had imagined a bottle of Bollinger.

"I decided to wait until I got home to break the news to Howard, knowing he'd be almost as disappointed as I was. At the time, he was between jobs—a chronic condition—so I knew he would be there. All I cared about at that point was having a shoulder to cry on."

Michael grimaced. "I have a feeling I know where this is headed."

"I've thought about it a lot, and I'm convinced seeing him in bed with another woman wouldn't have been as bad if it hadn't been my best friend. There's something particularly ugly about losing your lover and your best friend at the same time."

"What did you do?"

"As soon as I got over the initial shock, I threw my purse at Barbara. She screamed, of course, which I found strangely satisfying. I grabbed whatever I could put my hands on and fired away. It wasn't until I threw the antique lace pillow that my mother had given me that everything went downhill in a big way. The pillow hit one of the scented candles Howard liked to have burn when he made love, and it was like it had been soaked in gasoline. It exploded and shot pieces of burning lace everywhere." She frowned. "I meant to ask one of the firefighters why that happened, but never did.

"Howard panicked and started snatching everything that was on fire and tossing it off the bed. What happened next was inevitable. The bits and pieces of fire were like matches put to every piece of flammable material in the room. The curtains lasted less than ten seconds, Barbara's clothes on the back of the rocker didn't so much burn as melt. The drips fell on the rug. It smoldered and sent out a black plume of smoke before it burst into flames.

"I realized there was nothing we could do except get out of there and call the fire department. Howard had canceled the landline to save money, and my phone was in my purse, and my purse was still on the bed next to Barbara. I made a dive for the bed. Barbara thought I was going to attack her and grabbed me around the waist. She kept screaming over and over again how sorry she was, as if my forgiving her would put out the fire.

"Howard picked up his pants and tried beating the flames which, of course, fanned them and made the fire spread even faster.

"I've read stories about people who have gone through traumatic events and how every second seemed like a minute, but I never really understood what that meant until it happened to me. Every detail of those few minutes is etched in my memory."

Michael looked at Diana and gave her a wry smile. "You don't have to say another word. I'm willing to yield the most embarrassing moment contest to you. If you don't want to relive it again, I'll—"

But, surprisingly, she did. This was the first time she'd been able to talk about what happened with any sense of irony. "You might as well know it all."

He let go of her hand and put his arm across her shoulders, bringing her close into his side. "Okay—I'm all yours."

"We wound up outside," Diana said, continuing. "Me covered in soot and looking like a wild woman, Barbara wrapped in a blanket she'd grabbed off the sofa, Howard completely naked. Barbara and I started going door to door looking for someone to call 911. Howard tried to save his truck but couldn't get it out of the garage before the fire reached that side of the house. I tried flagging down a passing car. It slowed down, then the driver spotted Howard coming down the street covering himself with a branch from the boxwood hedge, and took off.

"We finally found a kid coming home from school. I scared the crap out of him when I grabbed his bike and demanded his phone. It turned out someone had spotted the smoke and the fire department was already on the way. Even so, all they could do when they got there was keep the houses on either side of mine from catching fire.

"I lost everything, all my grandmother's antique furniture, my yearbooks, my mother's wedding dress, the Christmas ornaments passed down through four generations . . . everything. Worst of all, I lost my grandmother's house. She was born in that house. Her father built it all by himself. He pounded every nail and put in every window and laid every brick."

"That's the kind of thing insurance can't cover."

"Having insurance cover *anything* would have helped. But, stupidly, paying the homeowner's insurance was a responsibility I let Howard assume when he insisted he wanted to pay his fair share. Of course that was when he was still employed. Afterward, he assured me he had enough savings to cover his portion of the bills until he landed a new job. He even made a point of telling me he would let me know if he needed help.

"If I'd financed the house when I bought it from my grandmother's estate instead of using my savings and a loan from my parents, there would have been a mortgage company to come after me to remind me to pay the insurance. But noooo, I had to show all my sisters and brothers how responsible I was."

"I can see why you felt you needed to start over someplace else."

"Sorry you asked?" She almost moved deeper into his

side when it hit her who he was, and why it was a particularly stupid idea.

"Sorry you told me?" Sensing the change, Michael stood and put out his hand to help her up.

"No." To her surprise, she really wasn't.

Chapter Ten

· · · · · · · · ·

THE NEXT DAY Michael went to work at the Carmel gallery and Diana went shopping. She'd bought a few summer skirts and blouses and shorts before she left Kansas, but she still needed work clothes and the Stella McCartney suit didn't count. She started at the Capitola Mall and then decided it would be more fun to try the smaller independent stores scattered throughout the overlapping towns that surrounded Santa Cruz.

She needed time and a lot of sales and careful shopping to rebuild her wardrobe. In Kansas she'd gotten by on clothes from her sisters, one slightly smaller, one slightly larger. It was nice to be trying on things that actually fit again.

Six hours after she'd begun, minus a half hour for lunch at a sidewalk cafe where she ate an avocado and sprouts sandwich, drank organic passion fruit iced tea, and thought about Michael's reaction to her story, she had five mix-and-match outfits that she could put together to make ten. And she was out less than three hundred dollars. Not bad considering only four items had come from the sale rack.

Synergy Organic Clothing was her favorite new store, although she loved the funkiness of Bunny's and Kurios. Pacific Trading Company made her feel like a native, and had clothes that fit so well it was as if they'd been especially made for her. Now all she needed was to find a great shoe store. She loved sandals almost as much as she did brightly colored tee shirts and short skirts.

Her severance had gone to pay off the loan from her parents. She'd used her retirement to tear down and haul away what was left of her house. The lot she couldn't sell, despite needing the money. Even her mother had told her hanging on to a plot of land without anything on it didn't make sense. But it was all she had left.

If she was careful she could cover the deposit on an apartment, feed herself, and pay her incidental bills until she started getting regular paychecks.

Things were looking up.

Tonight Michael was taking her to the boardwalk. Not her favorite form of entertainment, but one he insisted she had to experience to be considered a true Santa Cruz resident. To push his point, he tried to convince her there was a city ordinance that said anyone residing in Santa Cruz had three months to visit the boardwalk. After that, they would be banished to one of the neighboring towns.

She'd grown up attending rodeos and county fairs and traveling carnivals, flatland versions of the advertising she'd seen for the rides and games at the Santa Cruz boardwalk.

Her best memory of the State Fair in Hutchinson was her brother giving her a ten-foot long stuffed toy snake he'd won tossing baseballs. Her worst was throwing up a combination of hot dog, cotton candy, deep fried ice cream, and red velvet funnel cake at the top of the Ferris wheel.

Luckily, ten year olds are forgiven almost anything, and that happened to be the one truly cute year she'd had as a child. Her mother and father came to her rescue after being called over the loud speaker, grounding her brothers for a month as soon as they learned how much junk food they'd fed her. Once they were home, the month morphed into a stern lecture. Both brothers were on the football team and between homework, practice, and games, were never home long enough to be grounded.

Spotting a sporting goods store in a shopping center next to Highway 1, Diana pulled in to pick up a map of the area's running trails. The number was mind-boggling, the topography even more so, including everything from oceanside to deep forest to hillsides to flat tracks.

She took time to wander through the store and was fleetingly tempted by a pair of rainbow-splashed running shoes that cost almost as much as she'd spent on the clothes. A lime-green skort and a royal blue tank top caught her eye, but they too were left behind.

It seemed a lifetime ago when she looked back at how casually she'd spent money when she had it, especially on clothes. Howard had the largest closet, located in one of the back bedrooms, but the three she'd claimed provided twice the space. One, the smallest, was devoted entirely to shoes and bags.

She missed her old running shoes.

She missed her favorite hairbrush.

She missed her grandmother's afghan, the fishing pole her father had made and given her on her twelfth birthday, the ceramic cat with its right paw raised, that represented good fortune and money, that her brother had brought her from Japan.

Most of all she missed the dishes and embroidered towels and fragile baby clothes that had been handed down from one generation of women in her family to the next for a century and a half. If she'd had the insurance money she could have rebuilt the house and replaced the furniture and appliances, but nothing could replace the mourning locket worn by her great-grandmother's great-grandmother, who'd lost her husband and only son in the Civil War.

She had to stop doing this to herself.

Okay, so she'd lost a houseful of memories that she'd imagined one day passing on to her own daughter. They were things, not people. No one had died. No one had been hurt. She could make new memories.

DIANA PUT HER new clothes in the closet and dresser that Cheryl had emptied for her. She changed into maroon shorts and an orange and yellow striped tank top. The next half hour she spent on the back deck answering emails and texts and returning her mother's phone call. Her duty to friends and family accomplished, she tried to decide whether she wanted to be lazy and stay on the deck, soaking up the sun, or try out the closest running trail. Feeling herself leaning toward the lazy side, she changed into running clothes, strapped on her water bottles, and headed next door to borrow Coconut. She met Jeremy as he was leaving.

"Bad timing?" she asked.

"What's up?" he said, answering as if he been so lost in his own thoughts he hadn't heard her question.

"I wanted to see if Coconut was available."

"Sorry—she stayed home with Shiloh today." He opened the truck door and climbed inside. "Check back day after tomorrow. They should both be here by then."

"I'll do that." She moved toward the road.

He backed out of the driveway and caught up to her, rolling down the passenger window and leaning across the seat. "I don't know how much Michael has told you about Shiloh, but if she's at the house when you come by, she'll try to convince you there's nothing wrong with her. She might even try to talk you into letting her go with you and Coconut." He ran his hand over his face in a gesture of profound fatigue. "She can't."

Diana leaned against the door. "Would you rather I didn't come by at all?"

"No, she worries that Coconut doesn't get enough exercise." He sat up and put both hands on the steering wheel, then stiffened them in a forced stretch, a bone-deep weariness marking the gesture. "I know it's a strange thing for a twelve year old to be concerned about, but Shiloh isn't like other kids her age. She was excited about your offer and would know that I talked to you if you didn't come by."

"If I go slow, could she walk the trails? Or the beach?"

"Right now she needs her strength for . . . other things."

"What if Michael came with us?" she asked carefully. "Shiloh and I could sit on the log and watch Michael and Coconut chase waves." When he didn't answer right away, she added, "My father is always telling me that 'no' is a perfectly good answer. My idea was only a suggestion. I won't—"

"Yes," he said instead, warming to the idea. "She'd like that. She's crazy about Michael. I have a feeling she's going to be crazy about you, too."

The compliment surprised and pleased her. "I'm going to see him in a couple of hours. He insisted anyone moving to Santa Cruz had to get to the boardwalk as soon as possible." Why did she feel as if she had to explain the reasoning behind her and Michael doing something together? "I'll ask if he's free to come over day after tomorrow when he gets off work."

"Have him call first. There's no sense in wasting a trip if Shiloh isn't feeling well." A slow grin formed. "Never mind. I don't think he would consider any trip this direction a waste."

For the second time in less than a minute, he'd surprised her. This time she blushed. "He's just being nice."

Jeremy laughed as he shifted the truck from neutral to reverse. "No one who's lived here more than a couple of years goes to the boardwalk voluntarily. Unless they're hooked on the gelato."

"You mean ice cream?"

"Have a scoop of the vanilla bean while you're there, and then let me know if you still think it's just ice cream."

THE FIRST THING Diana did when she returned from her run was go inside to look for her phone. Thankfully, it was on the dresser and not somewhere along the trail. In the hour and a half she'd been gone, she'd received six voice messages and fifteen texts. She skimmed the voice mail numbers, stopping to listen to one from Michael. He'd called to cancel their night at the boardwalk, saying something had come up that he had to take care of, and asking if she was available the next night.

Until that moment she hadn't known how much she'd been looking forward to doing something dumb and fun . . . and to seeing him again. Determined to ignore the disappointment, she returned his call, reaching his voice mail. The message she left was too forced to come across as lighthearted as she'd intended.

"Hmmm . . . I love the 'available' part. As it so happens, I am free the next night." And every night after that, she could have added, but he already knew that. "Give me a call if you have to cancel again. It's okay. Really." *Too much.* "See you tomorrow. Bye."

Instead of returning the other calls and texts, Diana dropped her phone on the kitchen table and poured a glass of wine. She wandered from room to room, winding up on the enclosed back porch where she sat on the edge of a Mission style chair and looked around the oddly decorated room.

The walls were covered in an art deco wallpaper that looked as if it had been there since 1930. The floor looked original, too, not the factory oak that was in the rest of the house. Here there were expansion spaces to allow the boards to respond to the environment.

Something about being there drew her gently into another world, one of stories told in a whisper too soft to make out the words. This mysterious world enveloped her in an aura of peace and love so subtle that she doubted what she felt was real. How many lovers had kissed in this room? How many had made promises to each other that they knew they wouldn't keep? How many tears had been shed over those broken promises?

She got up and went to the window. An empty bird feeder hung from a hook on the eave, a sad looking finch sat on the tray. Waiting. Diana imagined him wondering what he had done that had made the food go away and brought such a dramatic change to his life.

Damn it. She wanted her life back. She wanted to be the person she used to be, the one who rebounded from being dumped by guys because she believed with all her heart that true love was out there waiting for her.

She didn't want to wait another year and a half before she took a chance again. So what if she still couldn't trust her instincts about men and met someone new and had her heart broken a third or fourth or fifth time? She would survive.

Raising her wineglass to toast herself, she saw that her hand was shaking and her vision had become blurry with tears.

She gave herself the moment, indulging in the sorrow that she'd learned came with healing. What she missed as she wiped her eyes was the sun clearing a cloud and sending a brilliant ray of light through the window. For just a moment, the ray landed on a tiny piece of sea glass.

Diana caught a flash of blue light out of the corner of her eye. She put it off to a prism created when sunlight hit glass. Easily explained. Certainly nothing magical or mysterious to mark a life-altering moment.

Overcome with a sudden sense of purpose, she took her half-full glass back to the kitchen, grabbed her purse and keys, and headed to the grocery store to buy birdseed.

Chapter Eleven

· · · · · · · · · ·

DIANA SAT ON a bench facing the ocean, saving their seats while Michael bought them fish and chips. She couldn't decide if it was painful or embarrassing to be so wrong about so many things at the same time.

First was the gelato, which Michael had insisted she taste before they did anything else. She sampled several flavors and finally settled on the vanilla bean. As promised, it was smoother and denser and richer tasting than any ice cream she'd ever had, even the ones in special cases at the grocery store that were so expensive they came in tiny tubs to hide their per ounce price. Best of all, it was two-thirds the calories of regular ice cream. In the simplest terms possible, even with the reduced calories, gelato was a distinct threat to the twenty pounds she'd lost in the past six months.

Second, she'd honestly believed she would be bored out of her mind at a boardwalk carnival. Seen one, seen them all, as her brother liked to say. He hadn't been talking about carnivals at the time, but it still fit.

She was anything but bored. How much that had to do with Michael holding her hand as he dragged her from one ride to the next, she'd save to figure out later.

Michael returned, balancing two paper plates and a tall glass of beer. He put the beer between them on the bench, then handed her a mound of deep fried fish and French fries. "Sorry—I could only handle one drink."

"I'll share," she said, smiling sweetly.

He laughed. "Well, that's mighty nice of you, partner," he answered in a truly awful attempt to mimic John Wayne.

"What can I say? I'm a nice person." She broke off a piece of steaming fish, and held it out to him.

Instead of taking it in his hand, he leaned forward and let her put it in his mouth, his lips touching her fingers. A flush raced up her arm and spread throughout her body like a flock of starlings fleeing from a hawk. With as much subtlety as she could pull off, she maneuvered away from him until she was sitting on the edge of the seat.

She struggled to find something for them to talk about that would put them back in neutral territory. "When Peter interviewed me for this job, he said you would be leaving as soon as he and your mother came home."

"Leaving the galleries, not the area. I've been hired by the Monterey Bay National Marine Sanctuary as an ecosystem scientist. The job doesn't start until mid-August, which left me free to help out at the gallery while my mom and Peter were traveling."

"I've never heard of an ecosystem scientist. What do you do?"

"I'll be assigned a marine species that's exhibiting unusual behavior, usually one with dramatically decreased or increased numbers, and try to figure out why it's happening."

"That could get pretty depressing."

"Not necessarily. But if it turns out the change is from global warming, we need to know how and why it's happening to that particular species."

"Is your brother a scientist, too?" From what Michael had told her about Paul, it appeared they were close.

Michael laughed. "He's about as far away from it as you can get. He's on the fast track to be an agent at the William Morris Agency in Los Angeles."

"Wow. How did that happen?"

"He started out as a grunt in the mailroom and then moved up to be an assistant to one of the newer agents. It looked like he was going to be stuck there until one day he walked in with Chris Sadler as a bargaining chip."

"The actor who owns the house on the cliff?"

"Who also happened to be a longtime summer resident of the house Jeremy's working on. He and his mom had June and my family had August so we never met while we were here, but the summer renters were a small group with a lot in common.

"Paul and Chris met at a party and got to talking. One thing led to another and they became friends. Since then Chris has opened a lot of doors for Paul. And Paul made sure Chris had first crack at the role that got him the Oscar."

Diana picked up her last piece of fish, started to take a bite, and put it back down. She was stuffed. "You do know all this food kills any possibility of getting me on any more rides."

"Which means we'll just have to come back."

She smiled impishly. "Wow. You'd really do that for me? Most impressive." *Ooooh . . . stupid statement.* She sounded like she was flirting with him. Which was something she definitely didn't want to do, no matter how much fun it was.

"Not to take anything away from that heroic self-sacrificing thought, but there is the gelato. I've been a fan since I was ten."

He'd saved her. And he'd done it on purpose. "Yes, there is that."

Remembering she'd promised her brother, Brian, pictures of the boardwalk, she took out her phone. Unlike her, he loved carnivals. He was her one sibling she knew she could count on to visit her in California, especially if she used the boardwalk as a lure. He was also the one sibling who would see the ocean and feel an instant connection the way she had.

Best of all, he would like Michael. She knew this as surely as she knew her mother would be a long time forgiving her if Brian came to visit and never went home.

Michael followed her as she moved to different locations. "You can get a good pano shot of the entire boardwalk from the beach."

She glanced at her watch and saw that it was a half hour to closing. How could that be? "Looks like it's something I'll have to save for next time."

"One last thing." He put his hand on her shoulder and guided her to the carousel.

"I don't know about this," she said.

"Come on—I've seen five year olds who went on this ride after eating deep fried Twinkies with a cotton candy chaser. Are you going to let them best you?"

"Now you sound like my brother Brian, the one who insisted I go on Ferris wheel after he'd fed me all that junk."

"Is that bad?"

She considered the question. "Sometimes. But you'd have to know Brian. He's my one sibling who thinks I can do anything."

"I can see why he'd think that."

She stopped to look into his eyes to see if he was teasing her. He wasn't.

I wish I could see it was the truthful answer, but it sounded pathetic, even to her. Instead, she said, "Brian has never cut me any slack. He's the only one who doesn't care that I'm the youngest and supposedly the 'baby' of the family."

He was the only one in the family who didn't commiserate with her when she lost the house. Instead, he'd been furious that she'd had such low self-esteem that she'd allowed someone like Howard into her life in the first place.

Michael laughed. "I wouldn't cut you any slack either."

"All right. I'll go on the ride," she said with no real enthusiasm.

Michael gave her a thumbs-up signal and went to get their tickets while Diana listened to the music coming from the throaty pipe organ. When he returned she got into line, and waited for the carousel to stop. As soon as everyone had cleared off, she started toward a gleaming chestnut horse with his head thrown back, carrying a blanket of yellow roses.

Michael made a grab for her arm before she stepped onto the wooden platform.

"Not so fast," he said. "There's more to this than jumping on the first horse you see. See that arm over there?"

She nodded.

"For us competitive types, the goal is to snag a ring from the dispenser and toss it into the clown's mouth. You get about a second and a half to do this, which means you have to be on the outside row and on one of the horses that moves."

"And if I get the ring in?" She was beginning to warm to what she'd always thought of as a ride for little kids.

"The clown lights up and a bell goes off."

"And then?"

"There is no *and then*."

"That's it? No prize?" She made a face. "I could use a new car."

Michael laughed. "Me, too."

She loved the way he laughed, free and spontaneous. She couldn't help but smile in response. This had been a good day.

Slowly, as soon as all the riders were on board, the carousel came to life again. She stood on the sideline watching the horses, immediately spotting two that didn't move and could make it hard, if not impossible, to snag a ring. She settled on a horse that had been patterned after a Lipizzan stallion, white with a black and gold and red saddle, its head tucked low, both front legs extended as if running at full gallop. "Okay, I've got my horse picked out." She grinned. "Now all I have to do is elbow all the little kids out of my way."

Diana didn't have to knock anyone out of the way.

Michael snagged the horse she'd chosen, and with effortless grace, lifted her into the saddle as if she weighed no more than one of the five year olds still waiting in line. He took the horse directly opposite hers, a stallion with its head up and teeth bared, sporting a red and blue and yellow saddle, with carved peacock feathers woven through his mane and tail, a true Black Beauty.

"You look like a knight about to ride off into the sunset at the end of a fairy tale," she said.

"And you look like the princess."

This time it was her turn to laugh. "Oh, gag."

The carousel held almost as many adults as children when it started. Diana turned her head, acting as if she were studying the upcoming arm that held the rings, but in reality trying to hide a flush of pleasure. Twenty-nine was too old to get this excited about tossing a ring into a clown's mouth.

Michael leaned closer to give her tips on timing and how to aim. He let out an excited whoop when during her first attempt, the ring made it into the clown's mouth without touching the sides. "You're a natural," he shouted over the music.

"I have two brothers who played any sport that had a ball. They made me practice with them every afternoon when they were supposed to be helping me with my homework." For the first time ever, she was grateful for all the times they'd dragged her down to the empty field by their house to make her chase balls.

The ride ended with Diana two bells and lights to four

misses. Michael lifted her off her horse, hesitating a second longer than necessary before lowering her to the wooden floor, turning the gesture into something startlingly intimate. He reached for her hand to guide her off the carousel. She purposely ignored him, stuffing both hands into her pockets and turning what might have been a simple courtesy into something painfully awkward.

The trip to the parking lot passed with inane chatter that Diana instigated and Michael worked to sustain. The car ride back to the cove bordered on agonizing. When Michael pulled into her driveway, he twisted in his seat to face her. "I hope you like it here."

Her heart did a funny little skipping beat. "I do," she answered. "So far."

Realizing how easily the last could be misinterpreted, she added, "Really—what's not to like?"

He stumbled over his answer, starting with, "I'm glad you're staying . . ." And ending with a simple, "Good."

"Peter's been calling me every day to see how it's going," he went on, then shifted in his seat so that he wasn't facing her anymore. "He said he'd fire me if you changed your mind about the job and took off for Kansas."

She hated forced laughter, but out it came, making her sound like a frog trying to throw up a bug. "Not much of a threat considering you're quitting as soon as they get back."

"What if I told you that I wanted you to stay, too?" he said.

No Michael, she mentally screamed. *No, no, no. Don't do this to me.* "I guess I'd say thank you."

He stared at her for a long time, his look unfathomable.
"Too soon?"

"Yes," she said softly.

"Then forget I said it."

Her eyes flashed a grateful smile. "Okay."

She met his gaze.

He wasn't going to forget.

And neither was she.

Chapter Twelve

• • • • • • • • • •

Michael waited until Diana was inside before he took off, cursing himself for being such an idiot. She'd told him in every way possible, short of sitting him down and writing it in the sand, that she wasn't interested in anything beyond friendship—with him or with any guy. What had he been thinking when he'd come on to her the way he had?

He pulled into the driveway too fast and tapped the brick wall Peter had installed to keep guests from going off the rock embankment.

Too bad there wasn't a mental retaining wall that did the same thing.

He-was-such-an-idiot.

With nothing or no one waiting for him, Michael got out of the car and sat on the wall, facing the ocean. This was his favorite kind of night here, a thin line of foam pushed ashore by lazy waves, an almost full moon the only light in a neighborhood where people were either in bed or deep into their own thoughts, a soft breeze that carried smells to trigger memories yet unformed.

The quiet was shattered with the hideous sound of Aqua singing "Barbie Girl." Whatever had made him think it was a good idea to keep the personal contact ringtone for Leslie that she'd put on his phone as a joke?

Leslie was the last person he wanted to talk to. "Hey," he said. "What's up?"

She was crying. "Can you talk?"

He could, but that didn't mean he wanted to. "Sure. Are you okay?"

"Yeah, I'm fine. I just need someone to talk to. Luke and I had a fight."

And she came to him? WTF? "Was it serious?"

"You're going to love this. He said I have a commitment phobia. Why does every guy I date want to tie me down? Why can't they understand I need space to be the me they claim to love so much?"

"You're asking the wrong person, Leslie," he said, his words tinged with frustration.

She came on point. "I thought I could talk to you about things like this now. I thought we were friends."

With stunning clarity Michael saw something in Leslie that he'd completely missed until then. "Friends don't do what you did to me, Leslie. You had every right to say no, and every right to be angry, but you had no right to make me feel like the world's biggest jerk for trying to show you how much I loved you."

Completely ignoring him, she went on, "Luke told me he

oved me and I told him I wasn't ready and he said it was because I was still in love with you and I told him he was crazy,
that I had never really loved you, and he said that I was lying
to myself and that I had issues I had to take care of before
he would even think of coming back." She stopped to blow
her nose. "I don't know what to do, Michael. Tell me what I
should do."

He was too stunned to answer. Instead, he did what he
should have done months ago and hung up on her. She called
back. He didn't answer. Next came a text. He ignored it.
Then came another call, followed by another text.

Michael put the phone on silent and laid it atop the wall
beside him. He jumped down, stepping from rock to rock, as
he made his way down the fifteen-foot rock embankment to
the sand below.

It was a perfect night for running on the beach. Low tide
meant that if he timed it right, he could ease past the cliff
that guarded the south end of the cove and run all the way to
Rollins Beach. Whether the tide was at ebb or flood when he
made the turn would determine if he came back the same way
or took the route through the housing tracts.

He managed to make it to Rollins and back in time to
see the first waves of the turning tide lick the base of the cliff.
Instead of wearing him out, he'd come home feeling fired up
and ready to face a morning that was still hours away.

He stopped to check the damage he'd done to his bumper
when he hit the wall. Luckily, it was only a minor addition
to the scratch he'd left the last time he pulled into the driveway too fast, not enough to make a claim—just enough to

lower the resale value. Before going inside, almost as an after
thought, he remembered his phone was still on the brick wall

As expected, he'd been bombarded with calls and texts
from Leslie. She must have been at it the entire time he was
gone, thinking she could wear him down. Assuming no one
but Leslie had called, he didn't bother checking his messages

HESTER WAITED AN hour for Michael to call her back, fi
nally deciding he must have gone to bed and that he would
get in touch with her in the morning. Michael wasn't the type
to ignore her call the way she had thoughtlessly ignored his
even knowing how worried he would be when he couldn't
reach her. He'd always been caring and thoughtful, the kind
of young man you hoped your daughter brought home.

But morning came and still no return call. Knowing Mi
chael always checked the voice mail at the gallery first thing
in the morning, she left a message there, asking him to meet
her for lunch at her house. What she had to tell him, she
couldn't do at work. And while it wasn't fair to put him in
the middle and dump everything on him, she couldn't wait
for Peter to come home, not with the new bookkeeper start
ing in three days.

Staring at the envelope she'd propped against the mirror
on the fireplace mantel, she clasped her hands together to
keep them from shaking. Every breath was an effort as the
crushing weight of what she'd done wrapped around her like
a hungry python.

There was enough money in the envelope for her to

disappear. She could get on a train—no one ever looked for someone on a train these days, it was all airports and rental cars—and ride the rails until she found a quiet town where sixty-three-year-old widows were accepted as part of the community, no questions asked.

If she just walked away she would never have to see the disappointment reflected in the eyes of the people whose trust she had betrayed.

But it wasn't her money. It never had been. She'd borrowed it when she was desperate for a loan none of the banks would give her, refusing to consider how complicated it would be to pay back. All that mattered at the time was being able to pay the doctor at the cancer clinic. Without the treatment, any hope of a cure for David would be gone.

What choice did she have? Her dear sweet David, the love of her life, the man who'd asked her to marry him despite her reputation as a hand-me-down from the football team, had flatly refused to sign the papers to get a second mortgage on their home. Selling it was out of the question. He refused to die and leave her in debt, and she refused to accept that he couldn't be saved. All they needed was a final fifty thousand dollars beyond the money Hester had already given them when she stripped her and David's retirement savings accounts and cleaned out their regular savings. She would have sold one of her kidneys to help him. Or, she would do what she did: risk spending the rest of her life in prison.

The treatments they'd been assured would save his life gave him less than a year. A horrific year. She'd finally accepted that the footbaths to remove toxins were a sham. The constant colonic irrigations perforated his bowel. The bizarre diet of vegetables and raw liver left him in a constant state of nausea. The mysterious mixture of chemicals fed into his veins, touted as being an alternate, supposedly gentler form of chemotherapy left him so weak he needed help getting from the bed to a wheelchair. And still the tumors grew and spread.

David begged her to let him go home so he could die in peace. Hester begged him to try a little longer—a day, a week, and finally a month. For her. She couldn't bear the thought of living without him.

He gave in and continued the treatments. And died a terrible death with nothing peaceful or gentle about it. The doctor said it was David's fault. Cures only happened when the patient had faith in the treatment, and David had stopped believing.

Hester was numb for months and then woke up. First she dealt with simple anger. Within a month the anger turned to fury. She filed a complaint with the Medical Board of California and followed it through the investigative process. She'd spent the entire past week, when she should have been at work preparing for the new bookkeeper, at the agency's district office attending hearings.

Feeling confident she'd done what she could to guarantee no one else would be scammed by the doctor or his clinic, she turned to the debt she owed Peter and Katherine. She was counting on Michael to help her. He would be kind because it was his nature. And he would do what had to be done because that was his nature, too.

She'd picked up the check for the sale of her house at the title company the day before. There was enough to cover what she'd taken, plus interest. It was the part where she had to admit what she'd done, where she had to look Michael in the eye and see the disappointment that would haunt her the rest of her life that she feared the most.

She'd planned it this way. It was cowardly, but she simply couldn't face Peter and Katherine. Not now. Maybe later when their disappointment had developed a protective shell of anger. They'd always treated her like family.

And this was how she'd thanked them.

Chapter Thirteen

· · · · · · · · ·

MICHAEL STEPPED FROM the shower and did a quick dry off before he wrapped the towel around his waist. The phone rang in the bedroom at the same time he was taking his razor and shaving cream out of the cabinet. Unless Leslie had started up again after being ignored for two days, he was fairly confident it wasn't her, which meant he probably should check.

He flung himself across the bed to reach the phone on the nightstand before it went to voice mail. Seeing who it was gave him a curious sense of foreboding.

"Hester—," he said, making no attempt to hide his surprise. "*Finally.*"

"I'm sorry I've been out of touch, Michael. Did you get the message I left this morning?"

"I haven't called the gallery yet."

"I wanted to know if you could come by my house later today."

"Of course. What time?"

"Lunch?"

He had a meeting with another vendor who hadn't been paid. "Around two would be better."

"Two?" She hesitated. "That would work."

She sounded exhausted, the way she had when David died. "I'll see you then."

"I'll make you those chocolate cookies you like. The ones with walnuts and powdered sugar coating." The words were followed by a hiccuped sob.

"Are you all right?" Of course she wasn't. "Do you want me to come earlier?"

"I'm fine. And two o'clock is perfect. If I'm going to get those cookies made I better get to the market."

"You don't have to do that, Hester. I'm fine without—"

"Please, let me do this."

She'd been gone an entire week and instead of offering any explanation, she focused on some friggin' cookies? "Okay. I'll see you then. Do you need me to bring anything?"

"No," she said softly. "All I need is . . . Never mind. I'll tell you when you get here."

DIANA STOPPED RUNNING and stood with her hands braced on her knees, gasping for air while her calves screamed in pain. Running on sand, even the wet packed sand along the shoreline, was a lot harder than circling the high school track at home. And it didn't help that she'd put in twice the distance she usually covered.

She took a drink from one of the bottles of water she wore on her belt. Next time she'd make sure Coconut was available. A dog that wasn't used to running on a leash would be a distraction and bound to slow things down to a more reasonable pace.

Despite her determination not to, Diana scanned the houses sitting at the top of the embankment, seeking the one with the brick retaining wall that she'd decided belonged to Peter. She was looking for Michael. She hadn't heard from him in two days and feared she knew why, she just didn't know what to do about it.

A summer fog had rolled in that morning, blanketing the beach and sending the usual sun worshipers inland to find other ways to spend their day. According to Jeremy, the fog would burn off by noon and the tourists would return. But for now, it was just her and the seagulls.

She started to leave when she caught a movement at the house she'd been watching. Even from this distance she could see that it was Michael. He was dressed for work in a brown suit and light blue shirt. The way he moved—showing confidence but no ego—took her breath away. She imagined him holding her and closed her eyes to prolong the feeling. Maybe this ache to be held had nothing to do with Michael. Maybe she just missed the feeling of having a man's arms around her.

She sighed when she saw him get into his car. He hadn't even sent a glance in her direction. She was invisible.

She wanted their relationship to go back to the way it had been in the beginning, uncomplicated. She hated the dance they were doing, where they concentrated more on making sure they didn't step on each other's toes than getting caught up in the music.

WHEN DIANA ARRIVED at the cottage, she wandered from the kitchen to the living room to the back porch.

As she had done since she'd first arrived, she stood at the window and stared at the world outside, a world that seemed different viewed from here than from any of the other rooms.

No surprise, she found herself thinking about Michael. He confused her. No, it was how she felt about him that confused her. Everything about him was wrong.

Since eighth grade, bad boys were the ones that had turned her on, the ones that made her care whether she was wearing underwear from Victoria's Secret or Costco.

Fluttering wings swept by the window. Seconds later a male house finch landed at the feeder. Instead of sorting through the seeds, he hopped to the edge of the tray and waited. A second bird joined him. A female. Diana smiled as they greeted each other and the male stood guard while the female ate.

Attributing kindness and caring to the interaction was considered anthropomorphism by people who simply couldn't accept animals had feelings. Diana refused to believe what she saw wasn't real. Even in a world of survival of the fittest, there was room for love. And there was room to feel loss.

How could she have had such a low opinion of herself that she'd felt lucky when someone like Howard chose her.

Chose her? She wasn't the love of his life, she was his meal ticket, until someone better came along. He'd cost her her home, her pride, and her dignity. Worst of all—she'd been a willing accomplice to it all.

FIFTEEN MINUTES BEFORE Michael was due, Hester parted the curtains in the living room to look outside. He was never on time, he was always early. Almost compulsively so.

She rearranged the cookies on the silver serving tray that David's mother had given them as a wedding present forty years ago. After today it would go into the box of household treasures she'd promised her daughter. Her friend, Josie, had tried to talk her out of giving everything away, telling her that she should wait at least a year before she did anything she might one day wish she hadn't.

Josie had actually cried when she learned Hester was selling the house that she and David had lived in their entire married lives. Her friends all believed she was leaving Santa Cruz because it held too many difficult memories. In one breath they said they didn't blame her for wanting a fresh start, in the next they insisted she should wait a year or two before taking such a drastic step.

She could and should go to jail for what she'd done. Nothing separated her from someone who broke into a bank or a house. She was a common criminal.

It wasn't right, but she'd counted on Peter's forgiving her once she returned the money.

If she was wrong, at least she was prepared.

Of course none of them knew the real reason she was leaving. She couldn't face them if they did.

Michael pulled into the driveway. Right on time—ten minutes early.

DIANA DROVE THE length of Ocean Avenue in Carmel twice looking for a parking place. Next came the side streets that were a reasonable distance from the gallery. Finally she caught a Mercedes inching its way out of a spot on San Carlos. There were benefits to driving a small car with dented fenders: she could get into tight places and no one parked close enough to pin her in.

She got out, looked around at the Mercedes and Jaguars and BMWs and decided it was wasted energy to lock her car. Because she wasn't in a hurry and no one was expecting her, instead of cutting across at Sixth, she wandered back to Ocean Avenue and looked at the shops.

With few exceptions, Carmel was not a tee shirt and ceramic mug kind of souvenir city. The one- and two-story business and homes looked Hobbit inspired. Quaint, picturesque, charming—all applied.

She wandered into one clothing store, and then another. This would not be the place she went to replenish her wardrobe. There were galleries and restaurants and wine shops and jewelry stores—all of them aimed at the upper middle class and above.

She was about to give up when she found the shoe store of her dreams. In addition to really cute shoes, there were handcrafted bags and scarves, some actually in her price range.

If she spent just one lunch hour shopping, out of the two days a week she would be working in Carmel, it would be fifty-five minutes more than she needed to get into trouble. Slowly, purposefully, she wandered back to San Carlos Street to the gallery.

The building was old brick and tan stucco, with a heavy wooden door painted a dark burnt orange. Mullioned windows were outlined in the same color. Pink and red and blue flowers spilled out of planters on either side of the walkway, and a simple brass plate embedded in the stucco contained the only indication that the Peter Wylie Gallery was inside.

As subtly as she could, Diana removed her phone and took a picture to send her mother. What was on the website really didn't do the gallery justice.

A bell chimed when Diana opened the door, triggering a smile from a middle-aged man sitting at a desk working on a laptop. He stood. "Good afternoon. Please feel free to look around, and let me know if you have any questions."

"Thank you," Diana said. "I was hoping to see Michael, if he's available."

The man frowned. "Was he expecting you?"

"No, I just thought I'd stop by." She smiled. "I'm the new bookkeeper."

"Ah—Miss Wagnor." He held out his hand. "Thomas Hardy—no relation to the writer. I've been looking forward to meeting you."

"Diana, please."

"Diana it is." He nodded. "I'm sorry, but Michael didn't

say when—or if—he would return today. He's at a meeting. I'm afraid you may have come all this way for nothing." When she didn't say anything right away, he went on, "I could call him for you, if you'd like."

"No, thank you. I don't want to disturb him." More disappointed than she wanted to let on, she moved to leave. "Would it be all right if I looked around?"

"Certainly."

"Could you show me where I'll be working?"

"Of course. I should have suggested it." He led her to the back of the showroom and into a small, thoughtfully decorated office. To make up for the lack of windows, hidden lighting poured from behind the cleverly constructed crown moulding. The walls were painted a soft yellow, with pillows covered in vibrant blues, greens, and pinks propped on the two oversize chairs opposite the desk. Two file cabinets, one a bright yellow, the other a soft gray, sat side by side on the back wall. The office was a world apart from the cubicle she'd worked in for the past six-and-a-half years.

"It's wonderful," she said. "Can I try the chair?"

He hesitated before answering. "I've been told not to say anything to any of our vendors, but since this directly involves you, it seems foolish to make you wait to find out." He cleared his throat. "Hester has decided to leave early. Basically, the job is yours to start at your convenience."

"She's not coming back? Ever?"

"That's my understanding."

Diana had counted on Hester for a quick review on the way she operated, and to go over any quirks about the people she dealt with. "Did she leave anything for me?"

He gave her a puzzled look. "Like?"

"A list of passwords?"

"I assume you mean for places like the bank?"

"And any other accounts that require them."

Thomas reached around her and opened an unlocked desk drawer. He took out a yellowed piece of laminated paper and handed it to her. "As far as I know, they're all right here."

Alarms loud enough to send an entire city scrambling to take cover in basements went off in Diana. Only this had nothing to do with a tornado. She glanced at her watch. With forced casualness, she said, "Since I'm here, and it's only a couple of days until I'm official, I might as well get started." Realizing she might be putting Thomas in an awkward position, she added, "Is that okay?"

He hesitated and then shrugged. "I don't know why not. As I said, Hester doesn't work here anymore, so she's not going to care. And it's not as if we haven't been expecting you." The doorbell chimed. "Michael will be glad there's someone he can count on. I'm sure you know, this has been a bad year for Hester." He moved toward the door. "I'll be right outside if you need anything or have any other questions."

Diana eased into the chair behind the desk. It fit her as if it had been made for her. Good thing. She had a sick feeling she was going to be spending a lot of time sitting in front of the ancient Apple computer. Somewhere in there was the key to finding out what the hell had put a successful business into a nosedive in less than a year.

She didn't like the obvious answer, especially with the way Peter and Michael felt about Hester.

Chapter Fourteen

• • • • • • • •

MICHAEL STAYED WITH Hester the rest of the afternoon and into the evening, listening as she relived her fight to save David. She insisted he know what she'd done out of desperation, and how she'd done it. Michael let her talk without telling her that Peter should have been there to hear her confession, not him. Peter was the only one who could give her the forgiveness she so desperately needed.

When Michael finally left, he felt as exhausted as Hester looked. Having his and Peter's suspicions confirmed didn't make what would come next any easier. But first he had to deal with Diana. From that moment on, his primary goal would be to get her as far away from the fallout as possible, even if she wound up going back to Kansas, and Peter had to find another bookkeeper. Just considering that possibility was like a punch to the gut. He no more wanted Diana to leave than he wanted to see Hester in jail.

DIANA WAS DEEP into following the money trail that had thrown the Santa Cruz gallery into near financial ruin, and didn't hear the bell signaling someone had entered the showroom. She'd skipped lunch and then dinner, declining Thomas's offer to bring her a sandwich, and then later, sushi. She had, however, accepted coffee. Too much coffee. Now, either hunger or caffeine had her feeling light-headed.

A simple comparison between the previous year's balance sheets and the current year's was all Diana had needed to figure out that Hester was the reason the Santa Cruz gallery was in trouble. She was a thief. And not a very clever one. On top of that, she wasn't a very good bookkeeper.

Diana and Peter were going to have a long talk when he got back. Trust was something you put in your wife or your friends, not your bookkeeper. It was a disservice on both ends. From then on, Diana would insist an outside accountant went over the books on a quarterly basis.

Hester's clumsy embezzlement would have been caught by a first-year accounting student. If Peter had just gone over the books occasionally he would have noticed the anomaly. There were new vendors, paid in even amounts, and haphazardly, without filed receipts to match the billings. Finally, Diana went online and opened the bank statements, studying the scanned copies of the checks. Her heart sunk when her suspicions were confirmed. While the checkbook listed a list of fictional vendors, all of the checks had been made out to, and signed by, Hester.

A feeling came over her that she was no longer alone. She glanced up, expecting Thomas with more coffee. Instead she saw Michael standing in the doorway, his arms crossed, leaning heavily against the oak frame. He looked awful, a somber combination of exhaustion, anger, and sorrow. She tossed her pencil on the desk, and leaned back in the chair. "You knew, didn't you?"

"I suspected."

"For how long?"

"I started putting things together a couple of weeks after I got here."

"And Peter?"

"What he knows about bookkeeping you could write on a postcard and still have room for a return address."

"Why didn't you say something? Why didn't you *do* something?"

"I did. I told Peter that I didn't believe Hester was leaving because she had this sudden urge to move to Oregon to be with her sister. Something else was going on. He said he would take care of it when he got back.

"But then he gave you the wrong starting date, and you showed up early and we had to figure out how to keep you out of what was going on. The most important thing shifted from protecting Hester to protecting you."

She pushed away her chair from the desk and stood. "I don't understand why you thought I'd need to be protected."

"Because once you figured out what was going on, you'd know that a crime had been committed. Peter was prepared to do whatever it took to keep Hester from being arrested. That left you in the middle."

Diana's frown turned into a slow smile as she filled in the

blanks. They thought that if she knew, she'd become an accessory. "How were you planning to keep me away from the books?"

"Bribery."

She nodded. "And how were you planning to bribe me without my knowing what was going on?"

"By offering you the apartment at the gallery. Peter figured you wouldn't mind waiting to start work if you had something to keep you busy, like getting the apartment ready to move into as soon as Cheryl and Andrew came home. I was supposed to tell you that Hester had requested another week to tie up some loose ends before Peter came back."

"And I ruined it all by showing up today."

"I told Peter it was a stupid idea, but he insisted you wouldn't mind when you found out later. As long as we did what we could to keep you out of it." Michael shrugged, forsaking his attempt to make their idiotic plan sound better than it was.

The corner of her mouth twitched with an unformed smile. "What if I told you that none of this was necessary? Would that take the offer of the apartment off the table?"

Michael ran his hand across his face and then through his hair. "What am I missing?"

"Embezzlement happens all the time. It's a crime of need and opportunity that's rarely practiced by hardened criminals. Few prosecutors want anything to do with it."

"You mean—"

"You and Peter, and probably Hester, have wasted a lot of sleepless nights worrying about this. If Peter doesn't want to pursue it, then it's over. My recommendation would be to let Hester set up some kind of payment schedule to return what she stole as quickly as she can. It will go a long way to help both of them make the best of a sad situation. They've been together a long time. My guess is that neither of them wants it to end this way."

Michael pulled out an envelope from his jacket pocket and handed it to her. "They won't need to set up anything. It's all there. She only took the money because they'd used all their savings and David refused to let her sell the house to pay for more cancer treatments. She managed to convince him that the clinic was going to complete his treatments free of charge because he hadn't responded as quickly as they'd promised."

"Oh my God," Diana said. "That's so sad."

"The saddest part is that Hester couldn't see that David knew he was dying and wanted the treatments stopped. His one wish was to go home to be with her for whatever time he had left."

"Peter's right. She's suffered enough."

Michael came into the room and sat on the corner of the desk. "You're sure about the prosecution thing?"

"Positive. But just to be sure California operates the same way Kansas does, I called around this afternoon to double-check. And even if you decided to pursue it, there isn't a prosecutor anywhere who'd want to take that on."

He gave her a smile that was the best thank you she'd ever received.

"I could kiss you," he said.

Diana looked deep into his eyes, and was lost in the way he looked back. Her heart on her sleeve that he would say he was only joking, she whispered, "Okay."

This time the smile he gave her curled her toes. He reached for her hand and brought her around the desk to stand in front of him. Without saying anything more, he cupped her face with his hands, and with slow deliberate intent, brought her forward until his lips brushed hers.

She snaked her arms through his and wrapped them around his neck.

He kissed her again, this time with his lips parted. On the third kiss, their tongues touched.

Diana sighed and fleetingly wondered what he would say if she asked him if he'd ever made love on a desk. Instead, she said, "What about Thomas?"

"I sent him home."

She kissed him, long and hard. A soft groan rumbled in the back of his throat. All of the baggage she'd brought with her from all of the men who had disappointed her exploded like a balloon filled with brightly colored confetti. Mentally standing in the middle of the downpour, she closed her eyes, swept away by a wondrous sense of promise.

IN THE COVE, a three-year-old boy rode his father's shoulders up the steps from the beach, talking nonstop as he had for the past half hour. He'd fought going home the way he fought eating orange and yellow vegetables. It was their last night at the cove, his last chance to hear a mermaid sing. Tomorrow his father would take him back to his mother in Sacramento, and then disappear for another month. Or more. His dad traveled with his job, and the boy never knew when he would look out the window and see him coming. The boy spent a lot of time looking out the window.

The moon was as high as it could go in the star-filled sky. They only had to wait until the seagulls were lined up just outside the wave's foam barrier, waiting, too. And then the mermaid would sing. The boy knew this because it was written in the book his grandmother read to him every night before he went to bed.

He couldn't leave now, not when he was so close to hearing the music that would grant him a wish. It would be his fault if his mother moved away and his father couldn't find him.

A tear escaped the little boy's eye and rolled down his cheek. He reached up to wipe it away with the back of his hand, then turned for one last look at the ocean. But it wasn't the ocean that made him sit up straight and grab his father's chin to turn his head toward the house at the top of the stairs, it was a soft blue light the exact color of the mermaid's tail.

"It's her," the little boy insisted. "We have to save her."

The father laughed. His son's imagination was only one of the hundreds of things he loved about him. Already he felt an intense sorrow that as his boy grew older, their magical journeys would end. The father would be like Puff, the Magic Dragon, left behind by Jackie Paper.

"How do you know it's her?" the father asked.

"The color. It's special." He wiggled to get down. "The book says so."

The father stopped and stared. He didn't believe in mermaids or magic, but he believed in his little boy.

"Maybe we—" The words stuck in his throat as the light flashed and abruptly disappeared. "It's gone," he said, more disappointed than he could comprehend.

The boy squealed and clapped his hands. "She escaped!"

The man's knees grew weak. He reached up, grabbed the boy under his arms, and swung him to the ground. The practical analytical side of his brain refused to believe what they'd seen was anything more than a blue night-light.

But the side of his brain that rode with his son on a boat with billowed sail knew without question that they had witnessed something too special for words. Instinctively, he knew that this time the magic had been for someone else. One day, the magic would be for them.

*You're invited to revisit the beach house, as
Georgia Bockoven's Beach House series continues.
Coming soon from William Morrow. . .
Read on for a sneak peek at the story!*

And don't miss the other Beach House books!

The Beach House

*The beach house is a peaceful haven, a place
to escape everyday problems. Here, three
families find their feelings intensified, and
their lives transformed each summer.*

Another Summer

*The moving and powerful story of four
families, the conflicts that tear them apart . . .
and the house that brings them together.*

Return to the Beach House

*Over the course of one year, in a charming cottage
by the sea, eight people will discover love and
remembrance, reconciliation and reunion, and
beginnings and endings in this unforgettable novel.*

In the next Beach House novel . . .

AFTER YOU'VE GIVEN your baby to strangers, how do you answer when someone asks if you have children?

The beach house that has harbored and healed troubled hearts for decades opens its door once again for a powerful emotional story that spans an entire summer. The first lost soul who arrives is an achingly lonely woman who sees herself as little more than a placeholder in a life as empty as a champagne bottle at a wedding reception.

Fourteen years ago, Melinda Campbell was fifteen and a half, pregnant, and terrified the baby's father and grandfather would find out. Melinda's father, critically ill with black lung disease, sends his daughter to stay with her aunt until the baby is born. Torn between trying to take care of her baby or her father, Melinda chooses adoption.

Now, thirteen years later, she is living the life her father struggled to give her, college educated and moving up the corporate ladder in a state a thousand miles from West Virginia. Her cupboards are filled with food that didn't come from a food bank, her closet has shoes that equal her father's yearly income. So what if her smiles are empty or if she sees the world through haunted eyes—or if when she goes home at night her only company is a silver and white shelter cat?

Jeremy Richmond knows the beach house the way a painter knows his canvas, intimately and focused on detail. He is a strong-willed passionate man whose life revolves around his adopted daughter, Shiloh. She owned his heart the moment his wife, Tess, put her into his arms. For three years they were the picture-perfect family, the one advertisers use to sell everything from cars to cameras. Then Shiloh was diagnosed with pediatric lupus and Tess walked away, saying she wanted no part of taking care of a critically ill child.

Jeremy's life becomes narrowly focused between his contracting business and Shiloh. He convinces himself it is enough for both of them when Shiloh opens a door to a world Jeremy had no idea she inhabited.

With heartbreaking calm and devastating acceptance, Shiloh tells Jeremy she's tired of fighting her illness and wants to meet her biological mother before it's too late. Desperate to give Shiloh something to live for, Jeremy agrees to do what he can to find someone he has no desire to meet.

Bestselling author Georgia Bockoven is at her powerful and emotional peak telling the story of three deeply wounded souls who come together at the beach house. Distrust and anger keep them apart; only understanding and love can heal them...

About the Author

....

GEORGIA BOCKOVEN is an award-winning author who began writing fiction after a successful career as a freelance journalist and photographer. Her books have sold more than three million copies worldwide. The mother of two, she resides in northern California with her husband, John.

Discover great authors, exclusive offers, and more at hc.com.